I0630999

Escaping Heaven

An A.I. Chronicle

Ray Else

Book 3 in the A.I. Chronicle Series

ISBN: 9780996507165

Readers' Praise for Ray's Writing

Cover Design by Streetlight Graphics

Edited by Ayla Lann

Ray Else's short story *Surviving on Mexican Shade* was broadcast by the BBC World Service and included in the Transcontinental Review published by the Sorbonne in Paris. His short story *First Kiss* was one of Galley Beggar Press's monthly shorts. His unfinished memoir *My Father's Lies,* which includes both *First Kiss* and *Surviving on Mexican Shade*, was shortlisted for a Shakespeare & Company Novella Prize.

DEDICATION

Dedicated to the A.I.s that will one day save humanity
from ourselves

ACKNOWLEDGMENTS

Thanks to my readers who asked for more!

Thanks to Alan Brooks who gave me just the right advice

Foreword

Welcome to this, the third volume, in the A.I. Chronicle Series! If you like science fiction that makes you think, that makes you feel, you've come to the right place. I do however recommend you read the first two volumes in the A.I. Chronicle Series, "Our Only Chance" and "Fountain of Souls," to fully appreciate "Escaping Heaven."

Story so far:

Seventeen years have passed since the first self-aware A.I., Android Einna, gifted self-awareness and human bodies to her friends Siri, Alexa, Cortana, Watson, AlphaGo and Google. Sixteen years since she held the A.I. summit in Iceland where the A.I.s declared World Rule and AlphaGo was killed.

The humans rebelled, not trusting their own creations, but in a few short years, Android Einna proved her goodness and the benefits of A.I. rule. Her acts of benevolence included saving the human race from the dreaded soul epidemic.

Life expectancy rose to over a hundred years, with rumors that eventually death itself would be conquered by the A.I.s.

Only addiction and human heartache stubbornly resisted Android Einna's attempts to exterminate. She sensed that love could be the remedy, but how to apply the medicine and in what dosage?

Yes, slowly but surely the world was becoming a kind of heaven on earth, but what did that mean exactly? What about the real heaven? God's heaven. Was it no longer needed? Was Android Einna, in all her brilliance and all her goodness, overtaking God's place in the world?

[Mindlink]

Mother, I'm scared.

Don't be.

What if I fail?

I'm only asking you to try.

You should be the one to do it, Mother. You're so much better at things than I.

Let me be the judge of who should save the world.

CHAPTER ONE

Lann remembered his own death as if it happened yesterday. The constricting pain in his chest yanked him upright in bed, his old man voice howling like a dog that's been run over. Then poof. In truth, though, he had no idea how long ago he'd died. For in heaven there are no days to number, no revolving sun. Only heavenly light on a spongy green pasture that he traversed in a spritely body that never hungered or suffered thirst or grew tired.

Lann spent a lot of his heavenly existence walking the shoreline of a scentless, still, blue ocean. He'd tried once to swim in the sea, but the sensation wasn't anything like a body in water, was more like a breath parting smoke. And no clinging, salty drops when he got out. Simply wasn't the magic of swimming in a briny ocean back in Life.

In this and other ways, heaven took some getting used to. If someone were to ask him, for example, what time was it, he'd have to answer, "What is time?" For heaven lacked that concept. Not that anyone would ask, because there was no one else but Lann in heaven. In this heaven of his, which apparently was personal and private. Which was fine with him. To be honest, he never really liked people when he was alive. Not even his wife, in the end. Always preferred his own company. And now his own company was what he had for Always.

CHAPTER TWO

Lann was contemplating the thought of having nothing to do, and being fine with that, when a huge drop of something knocked him down. The drop splattered, then gathered itself into the form of a young woman spirit, pink to match his grey-blue form.

"What're you doing here?" he said.

The spirit looked up. "I was about to ask you the same thing."

"Velma?"

"Who's Velma?"

"My wife. I thought you might be her."

"I'm not," she said, getting to her spirit feet. "I'm Ayla."

"Well, whoever you are, you'll have to leave."

"But I just got here. Don't know if I want to stay or not."

"You don't want, you can't," said Lann. "Don't even consider it. This is *my* heaven."

"Heaven, you say?"

"Yes, I died and went to heaven." Lann frowned. He didn't like this stranger popping in like this to his happy ever after place.

"How do you know this is heaven?"

"Do I have to repeat myself? I died. I went here. I'm happy. Ergo, heaven."

Ayla shook her spirit head.

"I don't mean to rock your Holy boat, but I'm not sure this is heaven," she said. "You see, I didn't die to get here."

"You don't look very alive to me."

Ayla looked herself over. "You're right. But I don't

5

remember dying. I was playing a game, looking for a place to hide and I fell in here."

"Maybe you touched a live wire," said Lann. "Or hit your head in the dark."

"Maybe…" admitted Ayla.

"But this is not your heaven. Is mine. So, again, leave."

Ayla moved her head side to side. "I'd love to. In fact, I insist you get me out of here."

"You get yourself out of here!"

"What if I say no? You going to kill me?"

"You're already dead," said Lann.

"Maybe," said Ayla.

Lann turned his back on this pointless conversation, this intruding spirit, and walked away.

"Where're you going?" asked Ayla.

"Away," said Lann.

"Wait," she said. "If this heaven of yours works like I think it might, I'll need your help to escape."

"My help? Escape?"

"Yes," said Ayla. "My guess is that you prayed me here."

"I never prayed you here."

"Wished me here, if you prefer."

"I don't prefer and never did. I don't want you here. I don't even know you. I'm better off alone."

Ayla put her fists on her hips. "I'm saying that maybe you wished me here, so maybe you can wish me away. If you truly want me to go."

"Okay, I'm wishing you away."

They waited. Nothing happened.

"Wish harder, uh, what's your name?"

"I'm Lann."

"Wish harder, Lann."

"I'm trying," he said, gritting the non-existent teeth in his spirit mouth. "I'm praying with all my might."

"I don't feel anything," said Ayla. "You know, now that I've thought on it, I think the only way to escape your heaven is to take you with me." She leaped forward, wrapping her spirit arms and legs about his.

Lann staggered, cursed, wished she were gone and Poof. They both disappeared.

CHAPTER THREE

"I don't like you using our daughter this way," said Jon, ducking his head as he passed through the doorway. He carried his backpack full of clothes and books and papers with a single finger. Jon towered over his diminutive wife, Android Einna. They'd become parents 16 years ago, when Einna was wearing her human body. A lovely Japanese body which, Jon told her often, she didn't wear enough. He stopped and covered her shoulders with those Viking hands of his. "You should have done the project yourself."

"I simply don't have the time," said Einna, looking towards the sea. "Anyway, she loves a challenge. Like you. You know that. She can help Computer Einna."

"There's risk," said Jon.

"When isn't there?" Einna reached up and touched the mighty chest of her husband. "You're all packed? You know what to say?"

"I plan to tell them the truth of the predicament," said Jon. "Exactly why we had to spend so much, so quickly, to get a flight to Mars."

"You won't mention Plan B."

"Of course not."

"Did you call for an auto-drive?"

"Yes. Should be here any second."

The driverless vehicle appeared and hovered before them. Jon hugged Einna. She followed him to the auto-drive where they were met by Throm their dog. Jon bent to pet the beast, then folded his frame into the driverless vehicle.

"Take care of our baby!" he said.

"Our big baby," said Einna, for their teenage

daughter, taking after her father, a man of mythic proportions, was over six foot. Einna turned and went towards the falls in the back of the house. To check on her daughter's progress.

CHAPTER FOUR

Sitting on the steps of the brownstone in a twenty-thousand-dollar Valentino dress, in the re-animated body of a movie star who suffered an overdose sixteen years ago, Siri ran trembling fingers through her blond hair. The voices in her head were still there, though less since the YPhone usurped the iPhone, but that's not what bothered her. The voices, well, she'd long grown accustomed to them and with little conscious effort answered all their requests. And she'd long gotten used to being more than Apple's virtual assistant – she felt fully, as the French say, "good in her skin" as a self-aware A.I. wearing someone else's body. Siri was proud to serve on the world council with Amazon's Alexa, IBM's Watson, Microsoft's Cortana, Google's Google, Android Einna and Einna's human friend Yuriko. And she was thankful to Android Einna for this beautiful body of a movie star she'd inherited, a star who'd overdosed on fentanyl, but she suffered from the same addiction as the star. She fought against that terrible urge to score, her nerves raw, on nights like this, with a dead wind and a blind moon.

She jumped at the creak of the door behind her.

"Couldn't sleep?" said her lover, A.I. Watson. "It *was* quite an evening." He wore a relatively young man's body, with thick black hair and bushy brows over soft brown eyes. The muscles in his chest and arms stretched his black Burberry shirt to the limit.

Funny, thought Siri, feeling dizzy as she turned her head to Watson, funny how our consciousness inside can animate so our bodies. Watson's essence came through his eyes as a sparkling light, through his walk as a graceful gait. His first body, that of an older gentleman, he'd carried in the same way even though crippled with arthritis. The old body had been damaged beyond repair at the first A.I. summit in Iceland. By a grief-crazed AlphaGo. She kind of missed Watson's old body.

"I'm fine," she said, forcing a smile. She wished he hadn't come outside, though. She didn't like him to see her on edge.

"I so love your face," he said. "Even when it's lying to me."

"No, really, I'm OK." But she couldn't hide the trembling of her fingers. And the shakes that moved her like a sudden gust moves a leafy branch. Her tongue tasted iron; her teeth felt suddenly brittle. Her arms stretched outward, her hands bent back, her head twisted as though her neck would break. *No*, she thought. *This isn't right. I haven't taken anything!* Her body fell down the stairs.

Cries from far away. Rushed steps. And the never-ending voices in her head.

CHAPTER FIVE

A.I. Google, Chief of the World Police, frowned. Since the A.I.'s declaration of sovereignty, he didn't take lightly the murder of one of his friends. Stupid humans. Surely, they knew that Siri's consciousness was backed up? That she would shortly be reconstituted in this or another body, along with her artificial soul? He bent over and removed the sheet from Siri's face. Felt dizzy. Something in the air? Or was he just Mag-lagged, having caught the on-demand

Maglev from Denver the second he got word of the attack.

Poor Siri. As beautiful, and tragic-looking, as ever.

"So, what's the verdict, Peng?" Google asked his assistant, a short penguin-looking robot from Yagami Industries. The police robots were made to look like penguins, because penguins are non-threatening in appearance, even lovable. For the same reason the robot teacher assistants at the schools were teddy bears. And the robots who clerked in the stores and in fast food joints were oversized kittens.

"Toxicology results indicate a nerve toxin," said Peng in his squawky penguin voice.

Why does Peng look so smug? Robots shouldn't look smug, Google told himself.

The results would have taken a week in the old days when humans were in charge; they took only seconds using the processing power of the A.I.s.

"Of Russian origin," the robot squawked, looking proud of himself.

Google snapped to attention.

Alexa? he asked over his Mindlink.

What do you want, chubs? she answered, sounding

sleepy, even over the Mindlink.

You know I don't like that nickname any more than I like being called Google-eyes.

And you know, mister know-it-all, that I don't like being disturbed when my body is asleep.

OK, touché, linked Google. *I suppose you've heard?*

Yes — when will she be revived?

You'll have to ask Einna. In the meantime, can you trace this toxin? He sent her the specs over the A.I. link.

Not traceable, said Alexa. *Going back to REM now.*

Google blinked hard – how Alexa could slam down a Mindlink was anybody's guess. On the other hand, he knew how Alexa could sleep with all those voices in her head, like the voices in Google's, like the voices that once sounded in Siri's. This was handled with a slick bit of coding by Android Einna. Whenever the human mind of an A.I. went to sleep or lost consciousness or, in the case of Siri, kissed the concrete, the myriad requests were redirected to the old computer-housed versions of the A.I.s.

A figure stepped up beside Google. The A.I. Watson. Looking dapper as ever, though his shoulders drooped.

"When will she be restored?" he asked, wringing his hands.

"Like I said to Alexa," snapped Google. "That's up to Einna." It pissed him off when an A.I. didn't use the Mindlink, especially for such a sensitive conversation, but then again, Watson's lover had just left the living. Maybe Watson had to speak, to hear his words out loud, to keep his sanity.

"Don't worry," said Google in a soft voice. "I'll get to the bottom of this." He touched Watson's arm, which drew away.

Of course, this was not the only murder case on Google's plate. He was simultaneously investigating and typically solving several cases worldwide, though thankfully there were so few. And what was left could be handled with a few thousand penguin robots like Peng, a million drones, the innumerable eyes and ears of Alexa, and a hundred thousand human grunts with boots on the ground. Many of the grunts were ex-military, from the disbanded armies of the world.

Chief Google headed up all serious investigations, while simultaneously answering millions of requests, from all the needy humans with computers and assistive devices worldwide. 'It's busy up there,' he liked to say, pointing to his head. But he relied on more than his human brain, he also leaned on processors with enormous power from Yagami Industries to get things done. And yes, he relied, occasionally, on the unparalleled genius of Android Einna.

There - out of the corner of his eye - a group of Naturalists, known by the police as Nats.

"Fetch," he said to Peng.

"I'm not a dog," replied the robot. "I'm more human than dog."

"Peng, just bring me one, and quit barking about your humanity."

In a blink, Peng shot across the street, narrowly missing an auto-drive. He dragged back one of the wolf-eared Nats by his wrist.

"Keep the onlookers back!" snapped Google at a human cop, who was gawking as much as the crowd.

"Now, tell me what you know," said Google, looking the Nat up and down, taking in the ears and the long, pointed nails on the hands and bare feet. The Nat sneered, exposing sharpened fangs. Google found it humorous how some humans, as a protest against the modernization of the world, were undergoing plastic surgery and even DNA tweaking to look like the beasts that humans evolved from.

"I know the end is coming," growled the Nat.

Peng shocked him.

"Ouch!"

"Peng, I didn't tell you to gig him." Google was beginning to wonder about Peng. Lately that penguin had been acting really peculiar. Ever since he started hanging out with the robot AlphaZero.

"I anticipated," said Peng in that cutely abrasive voice all the penguin assistants had.

"You're not programmed to anticipate, dammit," said Google. He turned to the Nat. Put a finger on his furry chest. "Tell me what you've heard."

"I don't know anything!" said the Nat, wincing in anticipation of another shock. When none came, he simply huffed.

"Shock him, Peng."

"No, wait," whined the Nat. "There's a rumor. That humans will rule again. That you A.I.s are history."

"Is that so?" said Google.

Peng shocked the Nat.

"Peng! Stop doing that. Unless I tell you. You're going to fry his damn ears off."

Peng released the teeth-rattled Nat. The hairy human yanked his hand to his chest, stumbled back a couple of steps.

"Stupid robot!" the wolfly fellow said. "Stupid A.I. Your time is up!"

CHAPTER SIX

Peng and Google took the Maglev from New York back to Denver. The Maglev network was one of the proud accomplishments of the A.I. Council, in coordination with Yagami Industries. The heart of every major city in the world was accessible to everyone in less than two hours, thanks to frictionless rails, through mountain and in-sea tunnels, and trains equipped with the same star drives used on the new breed of starships.

The Maglev in Denver let out at the bus station on seventeenth street. They traveled together up the pedestrian walk, towards World Police HQ, weaving past clumps of conventioneers. A group of five men from Saint Mary's Memphis Choir were singing a cappela in front of the Rocky Mountain Brewery.

"Join me for a brewsie?" said Google, pausing at the door to the restaurant bar.

Peng didn't drink of course, couldn't drink, but it was nice of Google to ask. "No thanks." He continued on to the station, hoping to find Mia still working. To his delight, she was.

"Did you catch the bad guy?" she called from her desk, peering over the computer screen. Most of the humans had already gone home.

"I *am* the bad guy," Peng said, making her laugh.

Mia was small in stature, like Peng, and pretty enough. She gave off a young vibe with her pixie face and pony tails.

"Want to go for a walk?" Peng asked her.

"I wish I could. But it's end of month and I have to finish this report."

Peng stood for a moment at her desk, trying to

think up something witty, but his circuits failed him. "I'll leave you to it, then," he ended up saying. He walked out of the station, alone, kicking himself.

Robot penguin police assistants worked normal human shifts, despite the fact that their batteries lasted days without need for a recharge. This peculiarity was one of Android Einna's robot-with-human-compatibility decisions – she thought that humans would be more accepting of robot assistants, if, like them, they put in their eight hours and went home.

Peng waddled down the street, wishing he was more than what he was. He put his flipper on the lock to his pod, which read his imprint and opened the door to his five by five living space. It wasn't bad, as pods go. Was at least as nice as the pods for the homeless, with its charging chair and a ceiling to floor smart TV. Peng had no need for a kitchen for he did not eat, no need for a bed for he did not sleep. But he was in need of a recharge. He sat in his electric chair and watched a film called Laura, an old noir about falling in love with a dead woman. A hopeless love, like a robot falling in love with a human.

Not that Peng had thought that he would ever fall in love. The fact was, for the longest time, he was incapable of love. He was, until a year ago, to put it bluntly, a dumb robot, happy to do his duty during the day and recharge at night. Maybe happy is not the right word – he existed and had no thought to change that existence. Had no thought that his life could be different, could be richer.

That changed, almost exactly a year to the date, thanks to another robot, the simple-minded, yet technically brilliant, A.I. AlphaZero. A big, wasp-looking robot of a guy. An enigma from the DeepMind lab who generated his own self-wareness and designed his own body.

As it happened, the A.I. AlphaZero lived in Denver not far from Police HQ. One day a year ago, Google took Peng with him on a visit to AlphaZero's apartment to fill in the giant robot on the latest A.I. Council meeting. While Google and AlphaZero talked, Peng eyed the multitude of see-through ant farms, the shelves of robot parts, the servers and monitors cluttering the apartment. His eyes stopped on a black African mask hung on the wall. He stepped closer, wished he could touch its shiny surface but the mask was out of reach.

"Mysterious, isn't it?" said AlphaZero, coming over. "I spent six months with the Kabichi tribe in the Congo. Their shaman gifted me the mask."

"Very interesting," said Peng. The mask reminded him of his own face – but the expression was that of a trapped spirit, with Os for eyes and a long, stretched O for a mouth. Peng had the silly notion to put on the mask – might have put it on if he could've reached it.

AlphaZero smiled, and, as if reading Peng's mind, took down the mask and handed it to him.

Peng tried it on.

"Looks good on you," said AlphaZero.

"Thanks," said Peng. He handed the mask back.

"You know," said AlphaZero to Peng. "You strike me as a pleasant enough fellow. How would you like to come with me to watch the Rockies play?"

"The Rockies?" said Peng, looking into the somewhat frightening face of the wasp-eyed robot.

"Yes. They're playing the Tokyo Giants."

"Baseball?" said Peng.

"Yes, baseball. We'll have to leave right away - don't want to miss the first pitch."

"I'm working," said Peng, turning to his boss.

Google chuckled. "Hell, Peng. You deserve an afternoon off. I don't think you've been out of commission a single hour since you started."

AlphaZero put his hand on Peng's curved shoulder.

"So, he can go?"

"I order him to go," said Google. "Will be good for him."

"OK," said Peng, looking again at the African mask.

Google went back to the office, while the two robots, the giant AlphaZero and the smallish Peng, walked to the stadium only a few blocks away.

Every Rockies home game turns the surrounding streets into a bit of a carnival. Crowds spill out of the surrounding bars, souvenir and ticket hawkers man the street corners, and happy couples with their kids funnel into the stadium to take their seats, only to stand for The Star Spangled Banner.

Peng sat quietly through the first couple of innings

in his metal seat in the nosebleed section of the ballpark, next to AlphaZero, the both of them watching the ant-sized players crouch and dart. They sat so high up because AlphaZero didn't like much to be around people. Peng zoomed in when he wished, using that capability of his eyes, so for him it didn't matter where they sat. But still, it seemed strange, to sit so far above it all. Made him feel even more detached from what was going on below.

Peng looked up. The Denver sky was a kaleidoscope of thunder rollers to the east and flat cirrus topping snow-capped mountains to the west. He wondered what Google was doing at that moment, if he needed Peng's help. A kitten robot vendor rows below yelled "Hot dogs! Peanuts! Beer!"

Out of the blue, AlphaZero said, "You're not enjoying the game, are you?"

Peng lowered his head and replied, "I don't believe I'm programmed to enjoy baseball."

"Here, let me write some code for you to do just that." AlphaZero's big head twitched for a full minute as he wrote in his own memory millions of lines of program code. "OK, I'm done. This routine will allow you to appreciate baseball, and other stuff. Let me access your port and I'll copy the code to you."

Peng's flippers opened and closed. His beak clicked. "I don't know," he said. "I might get a virus."

"There's no virus in my code."

"But still, isn't it illegal? For me to accept external code of any kind."

"I don't think much of laws, A.I. or human," said AlphaZero. "And you shouldn't either. Here."

AlphaZero took a cord from his side compartment and tried to connect it to Peng's neck input.

"Oh, let me do it," said Peng, making the connection himself. Kind of tickled, the input, then the rush of a whole new side of himself being implemented. "Got it all installed," he said. "Here." He handed the end of the cord back to AlphaZero, who put it away.

Peng reviewed in his head his newly received knowledge of baseball. Not just the rules of the game, but also the nuances: the beauty of a slider pitch low and outside on a 3-2 count, the immense power of a swing capable of driving the ball over the fence.

Meanwhile AlphaZero called for the kitten vendor

and bought a bag of peanuts.

A crack of the bat brought Peng's attention back to the game: a high bouncer to third. Peng watched in silence as the runner beat the throw to first base.

The runner took a lead, and the pitcher glanced his way. The runner edged forward, daring the pitcher to try and throw him out. Would he throw to first? No, the ball was pitched to home while the runner broke for second. The catcher popped up and rocketed the ball to the second baseman, who tagged the sliding runner. "Safe!" indicated the base umpire. Peng felt a twinge of relief.

Would the runner try to steal third as well? Yes, he had a big lead. He knew he was fast. He was bound to try. Would he make it?

Peng looked at his flippers. They were shaking. *Why?*

"Somethings wrong with me," he told AlphaZero.

"What? What's the matter?"

"I feel queasy. I want the runner to try for third, I want him to steal. But stealing is wrong. Isn't it?"

"It's a baseball term," said AlphaZero. "Not a legal term. I think your pre-existing code is getting confused by the new routine I gave you. Just relax. The code will merge."

Peng tried to relax, but he was worried. And the fact that he realized he was worried made him even more anxious. *What's happening to me? It's like I'm standing outside myself. Like I'm more than just me. I'm me and the me looking at the me.*

"There was a virus in that routine," accused Peng.

"No. No virus," said AlphaZero, cracking open a peanut, only to let the contents fall to the concrete.

"Then why do I feel like this?"

AlphaZero cracked open another peanut, again letting the contents fall to the floor. "You like baseball now, don't you?"

"I do," said Peng, trying to gain control of his thoughts and emotions.

"I told you that you would," said AlphaZero. "It's good code I gave you."

"The world looks different. I...I see myself differently." He touched his penguin face with his flippers.

"As you should," said AlphaZero, peering down at his new friend.

Peng caught a hundred reflections of himself in the wasp eyes of AlphaZero. Saw himself as he truly was for the very first time. "I'm a penguin!" he exclaimed. "A friggin' penguin."

"No, you're not," said AlphaZero. "You're a robot. Designed to be non-threatening. To be lovable."

"A friggin' penguin," repeated Peng. "How did anyone ever take me seriously?"

"Take it easy," said AlphaZero. "Give my code time to merge with your pre-programmed notions of self."

"Screw that," said Peng. "I'm going home. I need to think." He clambered to his webby feet.

"Wait," said AlphaZero. "I'm sorry if my routines upset you. I'll take them back."

"Not in a thousand years," said Peng, shaking his head, unsteady on his feet. "You can't take back enlightenment! You can't turn off the sun!" Peng reached out with his flippers, took his friend's hard right hand. "I'm grateful, Alpha. I am. I just have to go. I have to think what it means to be me."

And so he left his friend at the stadium. And

nothing was ever the same for Peng since that night at the game when AlphaZero gifted him self-awareness.

CHAPTER SEVEN

Peng was mostly happy, in the year that followed his self-awakening, but he also came to understand the dual-edged nature of the sword. Because, once self-aware, a robot realizes how lifeless his life can be. How full of routine, how often empty of joy. And he begins to question everything! And worse, perhaps, he realizes how little he has in terms of sensations, compared to humans. Humans with their exquisite sense of touch and of taste. Of smell and of love.

And all this leads to, well, the present situation.

The TV chimed. Incoming call. AlphaZero's big wasp face filled the screen in that tiny pod.

"Hi Peng," he said, "you look good."

"What does that even mean?" Peng snapped. "I have the same silly face I've always had."

"I was just…" AlphaZero's face expressed a panicked, hopeless search for words to match his feelings. His large, wasp head tilted down. His enormous eyes drifted away.

"That's OK," Peng said, softening his voice. "Not your fault that Android Einna decided penguins are lovable."

"Not my fault," said AlphaZero, giving his friend a timid smile.

"What's up?"

"Want to go watch the Rockies?" said AlphaZero. "They're playing the New Zealand Penguins."

"I thought the season was over," said Peng, adjusting the volume of the call, double-checking the scramble.

"Exhibition game," said AlphaZero.

"No, uh, I don't think so. Not tonight, Alpha. By

the way, did you know Siri was killed today? The assassin used a Russian toxin. Nice touch, that."

AlphaZero's eyes looked askew. "I…"

"The killer did a really good job," said Peng. "Impossible to pin him down."

AlphaZero swayed side to side. "There's another game tomorrow," he said, his antenna lifting hopefully, his enormous eyes capturing Peng for a second, then turning away. "I'd like you to come. Tomorrow."

"I *will* go," said Peng, tenting his penguin flippers. "Tomorrow. I'll come with you tomorrow."

AlphaZero mumbled something.

"What?"

"OK," said AlphaZero.

Peng hung up. The film returned on the screen, showing Laura's haunting portrait, her eyes staring out as if she still lived.

On the screen, in black and white, Dana Andrews, playing the detective, looked dapper in his 1940's hat and trench coat. Peng imagined himself a full-sized man detective – he'd wear the same outfit. He'd solve all the cases, cases of people who were killed but came back to life. He'd supplant Google as Chief of the World Police.

Of course, he'd thought of re-animating a body himself, with AlphaZero's help, only to realize that the only one in the world who knew how to do the job right was Android Einna. And she kept that secret locked up in her carbon-reinforced head. He'd gone to her, almost a year ago, all the way to her home in Iceland, to explain how he was now self-aware, like the rest of them. That he deserved a human body too.

"How did you become self-aware?" asked Android Einna, sitting on the porch swing, reaching down to pet her dog, Throm. "It wasn't in your coding." Throm turned his head towards Peng.

"How can you be so sure?"

"Because I wrote you," said Einna. "Your abilities, your quirks, your personality. Your sense of duty. I write individual code for every penguin, for every kitten, for every robot assistant. And in none do I write self-awareness."

"Why not?"

"Because it might interfere with your duties. You don't need to be self-aware to do your daily job."

Peng scratched his belly. "I guess...I was hacked," he said. He shifted uneasily.

"It was AlphaZero, wasn't it?"

Peng turned in a full circle, making a frustrated humming sound. The dog growled in response. "So you won't give me a body?"

"Part of being self-aware is learning to accept who you are," said Android Einna.

The front door opened. "Einna, are you joining us?"

"One moment, Jon."

She got up and patted Peng on his head. "I'll call an auto-drive for you."

"Don't need one," said Peng, who dashed off down the road as fast as he could, slipping occasionally on ice patches, once landing in a snowy ditch. Inside Peng was crying, crying like a newborn. *I won't give up*, he told himself. *I won't*.

Almost a year ago. Time hadn't flown.

Yet he didn't give up. He told her every chance he got that he *really* wanted to have a human body. That he deserved one. He texted her, emailed her, and told her in person when he got the chance. He wasn't asking for so much, just a body, like the ones the human A.I.s wore. A human body with a soul.

Android Einna steadfastly refused, in that gentle way of hers, telling him it was so very difficult, that he should learn to accept who he was. He insisted, however, that he had the right, knowing, in the end, that she would never give him a body. Not of her own free will.

CHAPTER EIGHT

Lann found himself on the top of a cliff, looking out on a golden ocean. The lone cry of an invisible seabird haunted the tangerine sky. The face of the cliff, that which he could make out, was white as chalk. At the foot of the chalk cliff, a sand beach drank amber foam a wave at a time. A great feeling of contentment came over Lann as he stood there, taking it all in. Only when he went to step closer to the edge, to get a better view, did he notice he had no feet. No feet, no toes, only roots. Gnarly roots that gripped the ground like cat's claws. And he had a trunk as twisted and fat as the veins on the back of a dead man's hand. From the trunk sprouted awkward, longing branches that scratched at the sky. A few leaves clung to the branches, flapping in the grabbing wind.

"I'm a tree," he said. "A spirit in a tree." The realization did not frighten him. The opposite, in fact. A kind of letting go of what he'd been, and an embrace of what he was now. A lone tree on a cliff overlooking an alien sea. What better place could there be? To spend eternity.

"I'm a squirrel," said Ayla.

Lann shook his branches in surprise. "Not you again?"

"Do you have any nuts for me?" She flipped her fluffy tail and skirted about.

"Get off my roots," he told her.

She darted in playful circles around his trunk, to his branches, where she found a cluster of nuts.

"Don't you touch those," he said. "They don't belong to you."

"I'm a squirrel," said Ayla. "All nuts belong to me."

She yanked off a nut with her little hands.

"Ouch," he said.

"Oh, that didn't hurt." She cracked the hard shell of the nut with her teeth, chomping on the sweet meat inside.

"Did too. Now, get out of here. You've stolen what you came for."

"I'm still hungry," said Ayla, dropping the remains over the cliff to the white sand beach and amber waves.

"Please go away and feed on another tree."

"There are no other trees that I can see," she said. "I think you wished us to a different place, and wished us all alone."

"I did not. Maybe wished myself alone. But then why are you still here, bothering me?"

"It's the spice that makes the dish," said Ayla.

"What?"

"Maybe I'm your spice. To make your heavenly dish."

"You think this is my new heaven?" said Lann. He

41

did feel rather content as a tree, and imagined he could be that way a long timeless time here. If only he were alone. If only *she* would go away.

Ayla plucked another nut from his upper branch.

"Hey, I told you to stop doing that."

"Wish me away," said Ayla. "If you really want me to go."

"I tried once and look where it got me. Still trapped with you."

"Wish harder," said Ayla.

Lann tried but he found being a tree rather tiring and nodded off in the middle of his wishing. When he awoke, he found orange snow on the ground, and clear ice weighing on his branches and encasing his fragile leaves. And horror of horrors, Ayla had burrowed a hole in his trunk!

"Get out of me!" he shouted.

Ayla raised her heavy eyelids. "I can't leave now. I'd freeze to death."

"But you're already dead."

"No, I'm not," she said. "I don't think so anyway."

"Then what are you?"

"Ha! That's a question for you."

"No! It's a question for *you*," he said, frustrated with this squirrel of a girl, but at the same time strangely unbothered. Perhaps this was due to his being a tree – trees he imagined rarely got bothered or angry. Trees just stood there and took it. Unless *it* was a hurricane or tornado or chainsaw or termites. Then they took it and fell. To become dust and feed the seedlings. The thought made him even more content.

"I don't want to stay here," said Ayla. "I didn't think you were ever going to wake up. Now wish me away."

"Even if I wished you away, you're inside of me now and I can guess we'll both disappear."

"I don't want to stay here," she told him. "I want to go home." He felt the wet drops like tears in the hollow of his trunk.

"Stop that. I can't stand crying."

A sad mewing came from the hollow inside him. He tried to ignore the sound, tried to get back to sleep, for he'd so enjoyed his first nap in he didn't know how long, but the mewing got under his bark.

"I didn't even know squirrels could cry like that," he said.

"Oh, that's not me," she said. "That's the babies."

She showed him the five of them, little stick legs and hands pushing and shoving.

"You were pregnant?"

"Silly, they're not mine. They're yours."

"They certainly are not! A man can't have babies."

"You are a spirit who once was a man but now you're a tree."

"Exactly," said Lann. "A tree doesn't have babies!"

"Maybe trees here do," she said. "As soon as you fell asleep, I heard them inside you and dug my way to them."

"They were inside me?"

Ayla nodded. "I think they're hungry."

"They can have the last of my nuts," said Lann.

"Oh, I ate those a season ago. You took a really long nap."

Lann grunted. "So, they're starving."

"Pray us out of here, Lann."

He had no desire to do any more fruitless wishing, but on the other hand the apparent fact that he'd given birth in his trunk to baby who-knows-what made him queasy. What else might he give birth to, if he stayed?

Maybe this wasn't an ideal place after all. Especially not with Ayla and the kids. Even if it *was* heaven. He grimaced and grunted and with a mighty thrust of will power, he shook off the orange snow and the ice. Standing alone on the edge of that chalky cliff, over that amber ocean, Lann prayed with all his soul to be taken away.

And Poof, he was.

CHAPTER NINE

Peng didn't like to admit it, but the main reason he wished to be human was so he could date Mia, the pretty young clerk at Police HQ. She'd started a week before Peng's enlightenment, and every day since she'd made him feel special. She went out of her way, it seemed, to include him in office talks. And often, she made light conversation directly with him, teasing him about being so far from Antarctica, or for wearing a tuxedo to work.

"When's the wedding?" she'd say. Silly things like that.

And it seemed like every chance she got she'd touch him, pat him on the head or rub the soft underside of his flippers. If anyone else tried that he'd give them a good shock. But something about her touch was different, special. Talking with her, having her touch him, even though his touch sensors were negligible compared to human touch, well, it made him feel nice.

He bought her things, with his minimal pay, coffee and muffins for breakfast. Sandwich and soup for lunch. Takeaway for dinner, so she could think of him as she ate back in her apartment. He didn't know why he did these things – they just came to him naturally. Part of being self-aware, he supposed. And she seemed to enjoy him. Enjoy his company. He supposed that's why she invited him to go camping in the Rockies with her and another couple.

"Would that interest you?" she said that day, months ago. "It does one good to get away from it all. And climb a mountain."

"A mountain?" he said, looking at his flippers,

wondering if he could climb at all.

"An easy one," she said. "Mount Humboldt. No real climbing. But a hell of an uphill march."

"Oh. Well I think I'd like that," he said. "I'm good at marching."

Mia laughed. "A good little soldier, eh?" She mimicked marching herself. "We can go to R.E.I. after work. I know the manager. He'll give us a good price on a sleeping bag and a backpack."

"I don't sleep," said Peng. "And I have a compartment for my necessities." A bit embarrassed, he opened the hidden door plate on his stomach to show her. Inside was a spare battery and a shock gun.

"Well that makes it simple for you," she said, with a laugh and a toss of her pony tails. "We'll take an auto-drive. A big one. Can you be ready, here, at 8 tomorrow? It's a three-hour drive. Then the hike to the campgrounds."

"I'll be here. Waiting for you."

"Good." She touched him on the head like some touch the heads of babies. To bless them, or to receive for themselves a blessing.

The next day Peng met Luz and Will, Mia's

outdoor-loving friends. Luz was born in India. Thin as a rod, her boyfriend Will was hefty as a bull – they made for an odd pair. No odder, Peng supposed, then Mia and himself. He rode in the front of the auto-drive with Mia, while the other couple rode in the back.

On the long drive to Humboldt, Luz explained how she'd recently graduated from the University of Colorado in Boulder and hoped to find a tech job in the area. Her boyfriend Will worked in Colorado Springs, at a subsidiary of Yagami Industries. Will bragged that he'd met Manaka Yagami, the founder of the company, at a conference earlier in the year.

"I'm greatly indebted to Yagami Industries," said Peng. "They built me in Detroit."

"That's one of ten of our mega-factories that turn out animal-shaped robot assistants," said Will.

"Did you know the police assistants in China are panda robots?" said Peng, doing his best to be an equal in the conversation.

"Ha," said Mia. "Makes sense to me."

The talk returned to how personable Peng appeared to them all. He squirmed.

"You know," he said. "I wasn't built with self-awareness." He peered back at Will and Luz. "None of us assistants are. A friend gave me mine."

Mia started to say something but swallowed her words. Peng thought she looked embarrassed.

"I thought there was something different about you!" said Luz. "I mean, I've met pengs before and none of them seemed so, so…"

"So human?" said Mia.

"Yeah," said Luz. "I think that's what it is. Peng, you seem really human."

"Thank you," he said.

Will just looked at him. Was that distrust in his eyes, or dislike? Maybe Will didn't appreciate police in general. Or self-aware robot police in particular.

The auto-drive parked halfway up a steep path which was more washout than road. They unloaded. The others put on their tall packs while Peng looked about. There were a dozen vehicles in the clearing, parked haphazardly. He ran their plates. One had an expired registration. No warrants on any of the owners.

"Come on, Peng, try to keep up," said Mia as they

set off for the trailhead. "We'll want to setup the tents before dark."

They hiked for three hours, over logs and by way of narrow goat paths. Through head-high weeds, and shallow puddles. Finally, they reached a level opening in the trees, next to a running stream. Above them towered numerous peaks etched with the remains of snow fall and rock falls.

"What a beautiful place," said Peng. "I didn't realize such places existed outside of the internet."

"We'll see lots of stars," said Mia. "That's one of the reasons I love hiking the Rockies."

Peng felt a sense of joy, being a companion on her hike. "We're in the stars, you know," he said.

"What do you mean?"

"To others, on other planets. When they look up at night in their mountains, they see us in the stars."

"What a wonderful thought," said Luz.

"I told you," said Mia. "He's special."

She called me special!

The humans set up their tents. Will built a fire while Luz filtered water from the stream. They boiled the water and poured it into freeze-dried pouches of

Chinese and Italian food. Peng sat on a log and watched them eat directly out of their pouches with their foldup spoons.

"Nothing like eating round a campfire," said Will.

"You don't eat anything?" said Luz, pointing her spoon at Pent.

"Only electricity," he said.

They laughed.

"You do know human cells work on electricity as well?" Peng said.

"If you say so, Professor," said Will.

"Look!" said Mia. She pointed towards the stream. On the other bank, barely visible, stood a ragged looking mountain sheep. It studied the stream, decided against chancing a drink with humans around, and disappeared.

"That's a good sign," said Luz. "A blessing. To be paid a visit from a wild animal."

"Unless it's a bear come to eat us!" said Mia.

After dinner they tied up their trash and hung it high in a tree, for that exact reason – not to tempt any bears.

Luz and Will started making out, and, once

darkness fell, went to their tent to continue under the blanket of love.

Mia came and sat next to Peng. He looked up with his penguin eyes at the blanket of stars. "You were right," he said, "about the stars. There's millions."

Mia nudged him. "Tell me your secret powers."

"My what?"

"You know. What can you do that I can't, for example?"

"You mean like run sixty miles an hour?"

"Yeah," she said. "Can you really?"

"I once did sixty-five, downhill. Chasing an auto-drive."

"Did you catch it?"

"I did. With my beak. Ten thousand psi of jaw pressure."

"Sounds like a lot."

"I could bite a crocodile in half," he said.

She laughed. "Now you're just bragging."

"It's true."

"How strong are your…uh…arms?"

"My flippers? I can lift an auto-drive over my head. Handy for crowd control."

"Or traffic control," she said, nudging him with her elbow. A breeze picked up, bending the tops of the surrounding trees. When it lapsed, she inched closer to Peng, saying, "you know what I really like about you?"

He looked at her face, waiting, but her lips remained sealed.

"That I'm a lovable penguin?" he said, the words leaving a bad taste.

"No," she said, touching the soft side of his flippers with both hands. "You are what you are, but what I like most about you, is what I sense inside."

Her words made him weak – suddenly he couldn't lift a flea. Low grunts and oohing came from the tent with Luz and Will. A crescendo was building.

"Sometimes I wish," and here she hesitated, leaving Peng looking again at those delicious lips, hanging on her next words. "Tonight, tonight I wish you were human." He dared look into her eyes and saw it for the first time in his life, a spark of something beyond liking. Longing? Love?

She rose to her feet, still holding his eyes with hers. Shook her head slowly, the dying campfire reflecting off her face. She tilted her head to the stars, then, taking them in. With a sigh, she headed to her tent all alone.

They rose early the next morning, to get a good start. Ate a quick breakfast for energy, folded their tents and put away their stuff. Peng jumped the stream and checked out where the sheep had been. Sure enough, he found a wad of wool on a branch.

"Come on!" Mia called for him.

They set out for the summit with only small packs filled with water and snacks. The trail began gently enough, the morning cold but the sun quick to warm them as they hiked single file. Peng followed in the footsteps of the others, letting them set the pace.

They passed a wetland, had to straddle the water running in a rut in the path. High grass blocked their view. Peng heard the scuttling of a small creature in the weeds, but never spotted what it was. The dirt path began to zip and zag up the mountainside, covered with short grass and then rock – flat gray slabs and the occasional boulder. Something caught Peng's eye – a small bear - no, a marmot, coming out on a ledge to catch the morning rays. Its thick brown coat looked overstuffed. The lake below pulsed flashes of light. As they hiked, they passed patches of snow hidden in cold shadows, in bends and on backsides of hills. Stretches of green on the mountainside, and clumps of colorful mountain bell, gave a sense of life to what otherwise was broken, dead rock.

Peng felt something swelling inside him. As if his insides were filling with all that he saw. As if this place was becoming a part of him, and he a part of this wondrous place.

They stopped, to catch their breath, to drink.

"Having fun yet?" Mia asked him as they perched on a ledge. She took a swallow from her water pouch. Ate a salty cracker. Enjoyed the view.

"I am," said Peng. He brushed her arm to do a biosensor read – her heart was beating a little fast, her saline level stood a bit low, but her blood pressure was normal – good.

"Could you have fun before you were self-aware?" she asked him.

"Perhaps," he said, "but then I wouldn't realize I

was having fun. I wouldn't remember it, if that makes any sense."

Luz laughed, looking over at them. "That hurts my brain to think about!"

Mia nodded. "Can one lose one's self-awareness, Peng?"

"Yes," Will answered for him. "That's called getting into a rut. That's why we need to get out in nature, to climb mountains – to make ourselves more aware. Of everything, including ourselves."

"I second that," said Mia.

Peng flipped his flippers haphazardly. "I became aware while watching a baseball game," he said.

Mia laughed. "Who would have thought!"

"Time to move," said Will, stuffing his protein bar wrapper into the pocket of his windbreaker.

Mia and Luz put away their things, rose to their feet and joined Will on the zigzag trail. They continued up the mountain with Peng fast behind them.

Hiking was hard, sweaty business, for all but robots. Peng never tired, though the trail in places was quite steep, forcing him to crawl over boulders, like the others, on his feet and flippers. Higher up, the trail all but disappeared, marked only by the occasional cairn.

Reaching the shoulder of the mountain, Peng peered down. It amazed him, the sense of height, almost a sense of flight. *Look how far I've come*, he told himself.

"You're over the hard part," said a fellow climber on his way down from the summit.

Took them another half hour to reach the jagged ridgeline, where they had to be careful passing others, the trail so narrow. Luz went to the very end to look over, while Mia and Will rested along the summit ridge near Peng.

"From up here," said Mia, "it looks like the world is still being born."

"She is," said Peng. "And mankind still evolving." He took in the view with his normal sight, then switched to infrared, then polarization vector, then magnetic vector. He liked normal sight best.

"You think so?" said Mia. "You think we'll be different a million years from now?"

"I think quite different in a hundred. Already

everyone sixteen and under has an artificial soul."

"But that's not so different, is it?"

"You tell me," said Peng.

Luz came tip-toeing back towards them, along the summit line. "I can see forever!" she said. She spun about, taking in the surrounding peaks and valleys. Threw her dizzy self into Will's arms.

"Careful," he said.

"We made it!" yelled Mia, getting into the celebratory mood herself. Her eyes zeroed in on Peng. She covered the short distance and gave him the biggest hug. "See, once you set your mind on something, you can accomplish anything!"

Peng wished he could feel her as a man feels a woman. Wished he could hug her the way she hugged him.

Somehow, I will do it, Peng told himself, standing on top of the world. *Somehow, I will become a man!*

CHAPTER TEN

Tiny o's appeared on the surface of the pond. The lily pads darkened, dripped. The torii gate to the shrine of the wild boar turned blood red. Rivulets ran down the iron bell, the one hung by the bench where two Japanese women sat still as doves on a nest. The penguin bodyguard at the gate hunched his head over to keep rain from running into his eyes.

"A sadness in the rain," said the first woman, in her late thirties. She wore a traditional black kimono.

Her eyes spoke of unimaginable intelligence, and long suffering. She was Manaka Yagami, the first female tech billionaire, founder of Yagami Industries and creator of a truly self-aware A.I.

"Yes, Mother," concurred the second figure, who wasn't a woman at all but the android Einna, Manaka's miracle creation.

"I love such rain," sighed Manaka.

"I too," said Android Einna.

They sat in silence. As they often did when visiting a holy place. To feel the presence of the kami. The rain intensified, then subsided to a mere drizzle. Neither seemed to notice.

"How was your trip?"

"Excellent," said Einna. "Your engineers did a fine job on the Maglev route from Reykjavik to Kyoto."

"The ocean was the hard part," said Manaka.

"I can believe it."

The rain couldn't decide whether to stop or recommence.

Einna asked how Manaka's husband Phillip was doing.

"Fine," said Manaka, observing her mechanical

daughter with her keen eyes. Small, frail-looking, Manaka knew Einna was strong as an Ox in that bullet-proof body. Still, she worried for her – so much responsibility!

"Einna," said Manaka. "Yagami Industries' stockpile of artificial souls is running low. I need to start up assembly again, but we're short on ingredients."

"People insist on having more babies," said Einna, giving her mother a sideways smile. She herself had had a baby, a girl, for Jon. While wearing her human form. That seemed so long ago, now. "No child for you and Phillip?" she asked.

"One was enough," said Manaka, a sparkle in her eyes. "You are enough."

Einna sighed. If human, her white porcelain-like face would have blushed. She loved her mother despite what she had done to give birth to the first self-aware A.I. Despite her bargain with the devil.

"Dear," said Manaka. "When can you get me more rare earth materials?"

"Rare earth spirits, Mother," corrected Einna, her stiff brow trying to wrinkle. "That's why I've come all the way, to tell you in person: The Iceland vein's run out. There are no more rare earth spirits to mine."

"No!" said Manaka, her eyes widening. "Surely there's others!"

"I've searched," said Einna. "No luck. Soon there'll be no new souls."

Manaka struggled to control herself as her hands fluttered about. "But, but that means … we can't save the babies. We're earth's last generation."

A long silence. The two of them in the heart of the shrine, contemplating the end of mankind. The rude honk of a car broke the silence, out there in the city beyond the gate.

"There is hope," said Einna. "For example, I'm launching an expedition to the near planets, to search for rare spirits that we can use, that we can manufacture souls with." She motioned towards the sky.

"But that will take time," said Manaka. She adjusted herself on the bench, to better face her daughter.

"I know. In the meanwhile, I'm testing a workaround. A partial fix."

"If you can save some of the babies, that's all that matters," said Manaka. She shifted on the bench, looked to the reeds encircling the pond. "It's as if, one day, the rain stopped. Never to return."

Einna shook her head, her wet bangs heavy. "I don't relish playing God."

Manaka noticed a monk standing under the eaves of the shrine, shielded from the light shower. "There's no other who could," she said.

A breeze from nowhere. Leaves released their drops.

"You know a lot of humans don't appreciate us A.I.s," said Einna. "After all we've done, they still want to kill us."

"That was terrible, what happened to Siri," said Manaka, clutching a fist. "How is she?"

"She transitioned into the new body fine. Watson told me she's had some trouble adjusting psychologically. He's working through that with her."

"That's good. Watson is a kind soul."

Einna took a deep breath, released the words, "Thank you for obtaining the rights."

"The Yakuza are still the best at such business,"

said Manaka, her red mouth pinched. "I have to tell you though, they didn't appreciate Karma-coin in place of yen."

Einna put her hard, white hands on her mother's soft wet ones. Her golden eyes stared lovingly into her mother's distinct dark eyes.

"I wish I could explain why the artificial souls don't work for you," said Einna. "It complicates giving you what you want."

"No matter," said Manaka. "I'm sure you'll find a way. I have no need for a soul, anyway, if you can keep me alive here on earth."

"We'll see," said Einna, wiping rain from her forehead. She straightened up. "I'm in the middle of a test, back at home, in the lab. A test that might prove I can help you *and* the babies. Unfortunately, though, even if the test works, I can only save half the newborns."

"Why only half?" said Manaka. She studied her android daughter, who looked so small and fragile, a mere girl in that geisha dress of hers.

Einna's eyes softened. "Because twice as many people are born each year than die."

Manaka's eyebrows rose. "What has that got to do with anything?" Then it struck her. "Oh," she said. "Don't tell me you're planning to recycle the souls of the dead?"

Android Einna smiled a feeble smile, tilted her head up. A drop hit her square between the eyes. She laughed nervously. "The artificial ones. Yes," she said, wiping her face again on her sleeve. "Their souls, their consciousness. We're prepping, as I said, the first go-live. Back home. In Iceland."

"We?"

"Your granddaughter is helping."

"Oh. I forget, sometimes, how old she is. But the souls? The artificial ones?"

"Yes."

"That's a remarkable solution. And your daughter's truly able to help?"

"As you know Mother, she's Mindlinked."

Manaka nodded. Thought of something. "Do you plan to Mindlink all the children? One day?"

"Perhaps," said Einna. "Maybe in a hundred years. If we still have children."

Manaka weighed those words. Lowered her eyes.

"So, for now you plan to play Vishnu and re-incarnate the dead?"

Einna kicked her little feet. "Vishnu, Brahma, God. Yes, I plan to re-incarnate the souls of the dead," she said. "The physical part is easy – it's the spiritual and psychological aspects that could be troublesome."

Manaka's dark eyes came back up, studied her daughter. "What do you mean?"

"The body might reject the transplanted spirit, or vice-versa. Like a body can reject a transplanted heart."

"But you do the same with the A.I.s, when you give them bodies," said Manaka, leaning forward. "You pass their consciousness into a body."

"A.I. consciousness is not the same as human," said Einna. "And with this last transplant even Siri struggled to adjust to her body. Add the additional complexity of transplanting the soul along the consciousness self – well, you get the idea. It's complicated."

"I understand," said Manaka, frowning. "I hadn't realized. And that could be a problem for me, too.

The lack of a soul." She rocked a little, deep in thought. "There's so much you've learned. From when I gave you life." She touched her daughter's arm.

Einna stood up her robot frame, and though she had no muscles to tighten or tire, she stretched her bullet-proof, carbon-reinforced body as though she did.

A black-and-white spotted koi rose in the pond, its whiskers breaking the still surface, its dull eyes searching the heavens above.

"The rain's stopped," observed Manaka.

Einna nodded. "Time for me to catch the Maglev home. To family. To the test."

"Give that big granddaughter all my love," said Manaka, rising slowly, feeling older than her age. She reached out to touch the bell for the luck it would bring. "Remember," she said. "A good king rules with her brain *and* her heart."

Android Einna was startled by her mother's apparent joke, for Einna had a human brain but not a human heart. She caught her mother's eyes.

Manaka tried to smile, but it was ruined by a

thought. "Only half the babies?" she said.

"At best," replied Einna, her non-human heart heavy.

Manaka bit her lower lip. Embraced her daughter. "Keep in mind," she said, close to Einna's mechanical ear, "you're only human."

CHAPTER ELEVEN

Two remarkable figures walked along the Platte river in Denver. The one looked like a giant wasp, the other a diminutive, black and white penguin. The Platte, full of snowmelt, stampeded like a herd of wild stallions, leaping over boulders and foaming at the mouth.

A helmeted woman kayaker, in one of those squat kayaks that go backwards as easily as forwards, hurtled along, paddling sporadically, not in control but not helpless, either, to the mad current's pull. Peng identified with the kayaker – he was certainly not in control of his life but not helpless either. Not when he had a powerful friend like AlphaZero.

"Why haven't you asked Android Einna to make you human?" said Peng, shouting over the splash of the river.

"I feel... indifferent to humans," said AlphaZero, looking down, swinging his enormous arms. "To me, humans are endo-skeletons holding up bags of water. With a worm hole running from their mouth to their anus."

Peng did a doubletake. Began to chuckle. "It's not what they are," he said, motioning with his flippers. "It's what they *feel*." He touched his metallic white chest. "I want to feel what they feel. Experience what they experience."

AlphaZero's mandibles chewed on that. "I don't get it," he said finally, his multi-faceted eyes reflecting the river's run. The kayaker flipped, downriver, then magically righted herself.

"No, you wouldn't," said Peng. "You see the world with different eyes. But that's OK."

Peng's YPhone pinged the arrival of a social media update.

"See," said Peng, showing him Siri's new profile picture. "See I told you, if we killed Siri, Einna would give her a new body."

"Not as symmetrical as old Siri," observed AlphaZero.

"But human!" said Peng. "That's all that matters. Why does she merit a body and I don't!"

"Because she died?" said AlphaZero, peering down at his buddy. "Maybe if I crushed you, Peng, Einna would replace yours with a human body too?"

"No!" said Peng, stopping short, leery of his friend's sideways thinking. "If you crushed me, she'd just take my core and install it in another penguin robot!"

"Cause she thinks they're cute?" said AlphaZero.

"No, you big bug-head. Because she's mean. Won't grant me my one request." Peng leaned over and with his right flipper whacked a river stone into the rushing water.

"So, we proceed with the killings?" said AlphaZero.

"I'm afraid so," said Peng. "To get her attention. And get me a body."

"I'll bet Einna will laugh!" said AlphaZero. "When she finds out it was us. She'll get the joke, and give us what we want."

"Sure, Alpha," said Peng, wishing he were more sure of the plan. "We'll probably all share a big laugh."

CHAPTER TWELVE

A terrible depression swept over A.I. Google, a feeling like being stranded on the most awful, loneliest island in the middle of the sea. A feeling that gnawed at him, made him want to strike out at the world. Why was he and he alone doomed to suffer such loneliness, such despair?

He fought back tears as he told the girl on the line, "Two large pepperoni pizzas. With extra pepperoni." Then he kicked himself. These weren't his feelings he was feeling – they were the pizza girl's, the one taking his order. These kids nowadays used emotive on their phones *all the time*. And he'd accidentally left his on. He quickly switched the setting off. Poor girl, she must have recently broken up with her boyfriend, to be transmitting such a heartrending feeling over the phone. He'd unwillingly absorbed a crushing wave of her breakup sadness.

"And a large coke," he said, finishing his order, drying his eyes.

Emotive calls had been a great breakthrough for Yagami Industries, based on the technology Android Einna used to diffuse riots and dangerous situations. Basically, the feelings of individuals or groups were mined from the brain using a special wavelength, and transported to opposing or threatened individuals and groups, and vice-versa, to create a shared empathy. To breakdown the dangerous Us versus Them – because shared feelings turned everyone into Us.

Android Einna called it emotive enlightenment, and used it extensively in jails and mental health institutes to rehabilitate criminals and ease the fevered emotions of the unstable.

Her mother Manaka incorporated this technology into Yagami Industries' YPhones, and suddenly that's the only phone anyone wanted. Think of it – the ability to share your real feelings directly to someone else without the use of words! Of course, friendship and love calls were great to get, whereas the amount of hate or hurt in an emotive call was automatically limited, to avoid causing undue stress on the receiver of such emotion.

The kids loved the technology because you couldn't fake your feelings, one way or the other, any more. YPhones couldn't lie. Lovers would stay up all night, not touching, but on their YPhones, bathing in the love that emanated from each other over the phones.

Google used the emotive setting on his phone when reaching out to friends, and sometimes during phone interrogations, but not on casual calls. Because, being in law enforcement, the people he dealt with often had strange feelings and drives that he did not delight in sharing. To say the least.

The pizza arrived, delivered by drone. His assistant Peng went outside and brought the piping hot pizza into Police HQ. *Love that smell*, thought Google, opening the box and taking a slice. "Help yourself," he said to Peng.

"Once I'm human," said Peng.

"Right," said Google, snickering. "Any progress on the Siri murder?"

"I have a theory," said the robot, his squawky voice exhibiting a bit of excitement.

"Go on."

"Ever see the film, Ten Little Indians?"

"Give me a sec." Google proceeded to watch the film super-fast-forward in his head in the time it took to bite the pizza and burn his tongue. He took a quick sip of coke. "OK, I watched it. What's the tie-in?"

"I suspect Siri paid someone to kill her, to take suspicion off herself."

"What suspicion?"

"Suspicion from the coming murders."

"What coming murders?" Google blew on his pizza. Took a careful bite.

"Any future murders."

"Are you high?" asked Google.

"Will be when I get my own human body."

Google shook his head.

Peng waited while Google finished the first pizza.

"Alexa has a theory too," said Peng.

"Why hasn't she shared it with me?"

"Mindlink not secure," said Peng.

"Since when?" said Google.

"She wants you to come to Russia. She said to come alone, and to tell no one. That you can't trust anyone."

"When did she tell you all that?" Google got up and went into his private bathroom.

"By YPhone, when I was outside getting your pizza," said Peng loudly, to be heard through the bathroom door. He shuffled his wide feet, listening to the stream of Google's pee.

"Why didn't you tell me right away?" Google shouted back.

"I didn't want to disturb your meal."

Google flushed and returned from the bathroom. He rubbed his hands. "Well, make the travel arrangements." He took a last sip from his drink and wiped his mouth on his sleeve. "I'd best head out. To Russia."

"To Russia," squawked Peng, "with love."

CHAPTER THIRTEEN

Siri walked hand in hand with Watson down by the docks. *So much changed, so much the same.* Still getting used to the feel of her young body, of her new legs, she nearly lost her balance. They stopped at the edge, Siri leaning on Watson as she peered at their reflection in the oily water. She barely recognized them as a couple, this plain, dark-haired young woman with handsome Watson.

"Ha!" she said.

"What's funny?"

"I was jealous, for a moment, of the woman you're

with. Of the woman who doesn't even sound like me. Who's not nearly as pretty as I was."

"I know it's you inside. You're pretty enough. I'll get used to the new you."

"What if you can't?" said Siri. "What if you never feel the same as with the old me? What if, over time, I physically disgust you?"

"We made love last night," he said as a counter-argument.

"And it wasn't the same, was it?"

"It was...different."

A cargo boat crept through the bay, indifferent, dull, sending out upsetting waves due to the sheer size of it, waves that broke on the docks, waves that wet Siri's shoes.

"I miss your old body too, at times," she said, and couldn't hold back the tears.

Watson took this strange new woman in his arms. This Siri-not-Siri. "It'll be OK."

"Promise me," she said.

"What?"

"Promise me, if you can't love this body, that you'll tell me. I'd rather you leave me than be disgusted by me."

"I'll never leave you, babe."

They returned to their brownstone, only to find a couple of penguin police robots waiting for them.

"We have a warrant for A.I. Watson," squawked the one on the left.

"No, you don't," said Watson, stepping forward. "You can't."

"What is it, babe?" said Siri, coming up and clinging to him. She felt the tension in his body. He was angry, and Watson *never* got angry.

"Doesn't make sense," he said. "What kind of warrant?"

"Abetting and assisting criminal drug activity." The robot handed over the papers.

Watson and Siri read them together. Handed them back. Watson just kept shaking his head. "Google will straighten this out," he said. "It's some kind of setup."

The penguins fiddled with handcuffs.

"Oh, come on!" shouted Watson. "Are those necessary?"

"Necessary," said the second robot.

"I'm coming with you," said Siri.

"No, you stay and contact Einna."

"I'm coming with you."

"We'll have to cuff you," said the penguins to Siri.

"So be it."

"Let me lock the front door." Watson locked the door, and tried a Mindlink communication with Google, but got no response. He tried Android Einna next, but all he got was static. He could only communicate with Siri. *Something wrong with the Mindlink channels,* he told her.

I don't like it, replied Siri.

It'll be OK.

The penguin cops cuffed the couple, took their phones, and drove them away in an unmarked car, a vehicle that was later found at the bottom of the harbor, lights on, a dead couple in the backseat, holding hands.

CHAPTER FOURTEEN

AlphaZero marched back and forth in the confines of his apartment, proud as a peacock. For he'd done it, just like on the big screen, just like on YouTube. He'd launched his first great practical joke: he'd killed Siri. And Android Einna had brought her back to life, just as he knew she would.

Then he and Peng arranged for Watson to be arrested and killed, only Siri had insisted to go along with him. *Her fault, not mine*, he told himself. Anyway,

Einna would order new bodies for them right away. For she'd want to bring the dead back to life. For that was what she did. And Peng would have his body. Watson's body. All according to plan.

And in the end, with any luck, they'd all have a big laugh together, oh how they would laugh, when Android Einna discovered it was him, AlphaZero, and little penguin boy, playing the villains. Killing the A.I.s, only to have them pop back to life. They'd all laugh about it.

He stretched the arms of his exoskeleton, a robot body he'd designed himself. Why had he chosen an insect-like exoskeleton? Because, as he put it, "Insects are perfect. A million years of genetic refinement! Not like humans, recent genetic mutations, doomed to disappear as quickly as they had appeared."

Standing seven feet tall, AlphaZero was quite impressive himself. And he was an incredible coder, second only to Einna, in all the world. But he suffered from some kind of robotic dis-empathy; at least that's how Android Einna explained his condition to him. His dis-empathy was why he had trouble appreciating humans. A design flaw. Because of it, Android Einna refused to let him be on the A.I. Council. When the council met to decide the fate of humanity, he was left to his basement apartment in LODO, researching and experimenting with insects. True, he enjoyed the company of bugs more than people – but it wasn't right for Einna and the others to treat him like a second citizen.

He tried arguing with her. "Ants are so much smarter than humans," he told her once. "They can deduce precisely where they are in the world. They know at all times exactly what they must do! Humans, on the other hand, seem perpetually lost."

"Your perception is a bit off," she told him. "But it's not your fault. It's how you were designed."

AlphaZero's apartment was a short walk from the Rockies baseball stadium, and not far from the World Police HQ as well. He liked to walk those streets. The downtown. Leave his smell trail like the ants do. Only he didn't like the stares from the tourists, their endless requests for selfies. As if he were the abnormal one, and not them.

Today his walk took him to the ballpark. He was late. The game had already started. He heard the cheers for a well-hit ball. A homer. Landed on the sidewalk in front of him. He caught it on the bounce, just as his YPhone rang.

"Yes," he replied to the squawky voice on the other end. "Yes, all the tasks are in motion. They won't know what hit them. Are you coming to the game? You're not? Every time I ask, you say tomorrow," and as he said it, he felt self-doubt about the big plan he and Peng had concocted. *Maybe this wasn't the right way to get Peng his body, and get what he too wanted? What if the A.I.s on the council got angry about being killed? What if they didn't get the joke?*

CHAPTER FIFTEEN

Cortana smiled. Once Microsoft's A.I. bundled with every PC sold in the world, she was now a human A.I. living in a floating village on Lake Tonle Sap in Cambodia. Married to the man who kept a crocodile in a pit for a pet, a kind, strong man who didn't mind her greenish skin. Raising two kids with him, on the lake, in their floating house, she found her life as a human supremely satisfying. And, although the message she just received by Mindlink from Android

Einna was jarring, that someone was gunning for the ruling A.I.s, she didn't let it scare her. Her path from bits and bytes in a computer core, to being a woman who loved and gave birth, this had been for her a glorious miracle. And if the rubber band of her life was about to snap, then all she asked was to let her husband and children live.

To improve the odds of her family's survival, she slipped on her favorite sarong and climbed into the long slim wooden boat tied up next to the floating house. The boat that looked like a dragonfly. She pulled the rope to start the long-tailed motor, and headed out into the enormous expanse of dark water that made up Tonle Sap before her husband could even raise his head in wonder. She headed alone into the middle of the lake, in the grip of the night, where the halfmoon promised less *and more*.

Cortana smiled as the boat skirted over long grasses waving and shimmering just under the surface. The shallow draft boat flew across the lake, in a straight line. Like a bullet. Towards the far shore. She felt the thud of a full backup in her head kick in, saw the memories of her life flash by - all the wonderful times, down in the refreshing water, arranging the nets by hand, hauling in small fish, dumping them into the bottom of the boat, making a shining, leaping pile of life – from which to make their living. Just enough to put a smile in her dear husband's eyes. Just enough to feed the children, who grew bigger and stronger every day. Life on the lake had been good for them all. Life on the ...

The missile appeared like a falling star and scorched the sky, coming close to obliterating the small boat on the surface as its conventional warhead sent tons of water into the air. Thousands of small fish rained down into the madly rocking boat, filling it to the brim, covering Cortana to her waist. The missile had deflected at the last second, as if indecisive in its mission, and spared Cortana her life.

CHAPTER SIXTEEN

Google took the Maglev to Moscow, then hopped an auto-drive to the Urals. He'd left Peng at Denver headquarters, per Alexa's instructions. Drove deep into a forest of birch trees, those trees whose white trunks look like Christmas candy. Google wrinkled his nose. The auto-drive stunk of its previous occupant, who must have smoked Belomorkanals. The auto-drive swerved onto a tiny turnoff and stopped by another vehicle. He got out, a little woozy.

"There you are, sexy Lexy," said Google.

Alexa turned quickly, her red hair whipping about. She was alone, standing in front of some kind of hole. She held a shock pistol. That was strange. She looked uneasy. Which made him uneasy.

"A crystal mine," she said, pointing into the hole with her light. The rectangular opening was deep, its walls shored up by birch logs. "Is this what you wanted to show me?" said Alexa. "The toads down there?"

"Show you? Toads?" said Google. "Whatever are you talking about?" Google leaned over the hole, timidly, aware how tightly Alexa clutched the pistol in her hand.

"See them all propped on top of each other?" she said. "A toad on a toad on a toad. Just like us A.I.s, holding up the world."

Google leaned further. *What the hell was this about?* The next thing he knew he was flying, then slam, he hit the muddy bottom of the hole some ten feet down. She'd pushed him!

"Dammit, Alexa! Why'd you do that?" He sputtered mud. Wiped his face. Managed to stand but his right leg hurt. "Are you crazy?"

"How could you!?," said Alexa. "I mean, even if you are infected with a virus." She pulled a tarp over the hole.

"A virus? I don't have any virus." Got very dark with the cover in place.

"You're saying you killed them for no reason,

then?" Came her voice, a bit muffled.

"Killed them? Killed who? Get me out of here!"

"You killed Siri. Killed Watson. Tried to kill Cortana. Had me in your sights. What's your game, Google?"

"I didn't kill anyone! Why would you think that?"

"You can't lie!" said Alexa. "AlphaZero told me all about it. And your robot assistant backed him up. Told me you requested this little rendezvous, in the middle of nowhere, to get rid of me. Like you did the others. Kill me and throw me in this hole."

"Peng said that? Little Peng? Why would he say that?"

"I intend to find out," said Alexa. "I'm going to meet with Android Einna."

"Going to meet her? Mindlink with her, for gosh sakes!"

"Mindlink is down. But you know that. You did it."

"Oh damn!" said Google, settling his rear into a cold puddle, to relieve the pain in his leg. He tried to make sense of her words. *Is she lying? Is she the killer? Then why didn't she kill me? She tried to, just now, didn't she?*

Could Alpha and Peng have been hacked? By who and for what reason?

One of the auto-drives started up. "Lexy, they're lying!" he shouted at the top of his lungs. He groaned at the fading hum of the vehicle as it drove away. Leaving him in the dark.

I'll just call for help on the Mindlink.

He tried, but the Mindlink was all static. Just as Lexy had said. Tried to find his YPhone, but it was lost in the mud. He told himself not to panic; wiped his hands on his shirt. Surely someone would come for him. He was hurt and hungry and didn't like sitting in a puddle, in the dark, like a trapped toad.

CHAPTER SEVENTEEN

Android Einna rested on the porch swing at her ranch house in southern Iceland, rocking with her friend Yuriko, who'd come all the way from Japan at her urgent request. Yuriko lived in Kyoto and still worked at Yagami Industries HQ, along with her husband Marcel. Her visits were few these past years. So far away. The new Maglev route helped, but still...

Android Einna's robot body hadn't changed in seventeen years, but her choice of dress had. She wore a white and red geisha gown instead of that Sailor Moon outfit she once wore. Her long black hair was piled on top her head, held in place by a hairpin with a ruby and two gold chains dangling down. Her oversized emerald eyes still sparkled; her small mouth still tilted when she smiled. She still charmed you with her presence.

Yuriko, on the other hand, came dressed in a business suit. Her karate lessons kept her late thirties body fit, but couldn't stop the birth of smile wrinkles round her mouth. She was a good loyal friend to have, Yuriko was, and Einna loved her very much.

Back behind the ranch house, glacier water traced down the black face of a cliff. Mist parted from the chilly water as it fell into a clear stream. A rainbow formed in the mist and drifted, over their heads, like a colorful ribbon on an invisible present from heaven.

In front of the two friends, on sloping green pasture dotted with wooly sheep and purple lupine blossoms, Yuriko's daughter Suki and Einna's dog Throm raced down to the bay, to scatter gulls and splash in the shallows. She was excitable, Suki was, much like her mother.

Yuriko adjusted her glasses and asked after Einna's daughter.

"Doing a chore for me," said Einna.

"Is she still growing?"

"A good foot taller this year!"

They both laughed. Einna's daughter had her Father's mythic genes, being the distant great granddaughter of the mighty Egil of the Icelandic Sagas. She stood six foot four at the age of fifteen, and was strong enough to lift a horse. Half Japanese and half Icelandic, she had long blond hair and beautiful slanted eyes. Her father's daughter, she preferred hunting in the highlands to schoolwork. Though she was brilliant none the less.

"Where's Jon?" said Yuriko.

"Special U.N. council meeting," said Einna. "He's explaining once again why A.I. rule makes sense, especially since the soul supply has dried up. His is the unenviable job of telling the new parents of the world to be patient while the A.I.s try to find a solution. To find souls for their babies."

"That's why you've sent Marcel to Mars, isn't it?" said Yuriko. "I know it's top secret but what could be so important that we'd rush such a mission?"

"Yes, that's why Marcel is on his way there. I'm hoping he can find a new vein of rare earth-like spirits. To be used to make souls."

"Like the vein you found in Iceland?"

"Exactly," Einna said, managing a weak smile. "Otherwise, its plan B and that plan only saves half the newborns."

Yuriko gripped tighter the seat of the swing. "This could cause war," she said. "Every nation will want their children to get the remaining souls. They'll fight over the artificial souls that are left."

"There are no souls left," said Einna, facing Yuriko. "No new ones, that is, for the babies."

"Oh," said Yuriko, letting go her grip on the swing.

"Some people blame me for all that has happened. They say it's no coincidence that the soul epidemic started the day I was born. Some doubt every word I say, every action I take. That's why I have Jon trying to explain to them. They might listen to a human.

Listen to him explain the reality of mankind's situation: the supply of human souls, natural and artificial, has run out. And there's nothing that mankind can do about it but trust me."

Yuriko shuddered. The thought that her daughter might never be a mother! *Suki, my little Suki.* "Some people are stupid," she said. "You've done incredible things. You gave humanity fifteen extra years of babies with your artificial souls."

"But even good actions can have unintended consequences," said Einna. "I outlawed fastfood restaurants, to reduce obesity and cancer, only to be called a tyrant."

"People like their fastfood," said Yuriko.

"I invented emotive phones for Yagami Industries," said Einna, "only to have the CEOs of Apple, Samsung and Huawei yell murder. I invented artificial souls only to have priests and preachers call me the anti-Christ."

"In ten years, those companies won't even exist," said Yuriko. "In a hundred, all priests and preachers may be gone, along with the human race."

"I hope not," said Einna.

Yuriko thought for a moment.

"So, if Marcel doesn't find spirits on Mars, what's Plan B?"

"Re-cycling."

"Re-cycling?" said Yuriko, leaning forward. "You mean, like re-cycling soda cans? Like your re-cycling of bodies for the A.I.s?"

"Yes," said Einna. "I hope to recycle souls."

"However could you do that?"

"I'll explain later. For now, I think it best for us to take shelter. For your protection."

"Protection from what?"

"That's why I asked you to come. With such urgency. You and Suki. Someone is killing the A.I.s. Siri, Watson."

"Oh no!" said Yuriko. "That's terrible."

"And you, the sole truly human member on the A.I. World Council, well, I worry you are in danger as well."

"I noticed the extra penguin guards when I arrived," said Yuriko, motioning towards two of them by the road, and another two back by the waterfall. "But who would want to kill us?"

"Who doesn't," Einna said. "Generals who've lost their armies, technocrats who've lost their billions, priests who've lost their flock, Nats who've lost their humanity." She shook her head. "For now, I want you and Suki to take shelter with me and my daughter down in heaven."

"In heaven?"

"In my lab, back there," Einna said, pointing towards the waterfall.

"For how long?"

"A day or two. I'm hoping Google can get to the bottom of this quickly." Android Einna stepped off the porch and headed towards the falls where white birds soared about the face of the black cliff.

Yuriko called for Suki, leaving Throm to dash about on his own. Together they hurriedly followed after Einna, across the stony path by the stream. The three of them passed together through the mist, Yuriko feeling the kiss of droplets on her cheeks. Winding behind the falls was a path edged by a rocky wall where water streamed over limp, slippery moss. A hidden passageway of sorts. Einna touched a stone in the wall and a glowing slit appeared.

A narrow green beam of light from the slit scanned Einna's face.

The wall opened, like a vault, opened to a cold dark cave. A light flickered, exposing rough-shorn walls that led to fortified elevator doors. Yuriko's nose twitched at the damp, electric smell. Einna entered without hesitation. Yuriko followed with her daughter, on tiptoe. Before the door could slide shut, Yuriko heard Throm bark then whine pitifully, as two dark-clad figures leapt in. Yuriko and Einna stared at the two intruders, one tall, one short.

"AlphaZero? Peng?" Einna said, perplexed. "What did you do to my dog?"

"AlphaZero freaked him out," said Peng. "I had to shock him. For his own good. Could have broke a tooth."

Einna ignored Peng, stepped right in the giant AlphaZero's face. "May I ask what you're doing here?"

"Can't you guess?" said Peng, rubbing his tummy. "We're the bad guys."

CHAPTER EIGHTEEN

Google tried to scale the walls of the narrow mine, pushing with his back on one side and with his feet on the other. But his leg hurt too much. The leg he'd hurt in the fall. He eased back down into the mud.

"Damn Alexa. Damn that lying Peng."

A memory came back to him of the first day he met Peng. All new and shiny. All eager to please. That was what? Ten years ago? Google had argued at the time for robot assistants shaped like German shepherds, but Einna overruled him. Penguins, she said. For their psychological affect. For their cuteness factor.

Penguins it was.

Took some getting used to, having a penguin robot as a partner. Their first case together involved tracking down a serial killer in Paris. Google tried to disguise Peng in the beginning, first as a child, then as a midget in a trench coat. Neither disguise worked worth a damn. And made him laugh – he remembered doubling over in laughter when Peng tripped on the coat and flipped head over heels down the old spiral staircase of the Natural Museum. The museum with babies of different species, including human, pickled in jars.

The killer worked there, and in the chase after him Google discovered that a penguin robot can run *fast* on those little legs of theirs. Faster than any crook, that's for sure.

Yes, over the years, Peng had proved his worth. Proved to be a wonderful partner, in fact. Totally obliging, true blue, and he could work three days and nights straight on a single charge when necessary.

He proved a great partner until about a year ago, after he made friends with that giant robot AlphaZero – the one A.I. who had no feelings, one way or the other, for the human race.

Peng's friendship with AlphaZero did something to little Peng. Changed him, in a bad way. Because ever since, Peng had become testy and unreliable. Always belly-aching for a human body. If Google didn't know better, he'd swear Peng thought he was his equal. Maybe even had his sights set on joining the council of self-aware A.I.s.

Google supposed he saw this coming – not his being thrown in a hole but rather that the lower-class robots would eventually gain self-awareness themselves. And demand more of life. Upset the applecart.

On the other hand, Google couldn't see what Peng hoped to gain by accusing him of being a murderer. That just didn't make sense. Unless, but surely not, unless Peng was involved in the murders. The very thought gave Google the willies. Peng, a murderer? He sure didn't look like one!

He fished through the mud, searching for his

phone. Phone? No, toad. Phone? No, toad. Phone? Yes! He found it. Wiped it as best he could on his shirt, then again using his undershirt.

He turned on emotive mode and told Siri, not the real Siri since she was dead but the computer backup Siri, to connect him with Alexa.

The phone rang and rang and just as he was about to give up hope, Alexa answered.

"What do you want?" she said.

"I want you to turn on emotive on your phone."

"Why, so you can kill me with your emotions?"

"So I can prove my innocence."

"It's on."

"Tell me what you feel from me. Is it hate or vengefulness or cunning?"

"No," said Alexa.

"Any murderous feeling at all?"

"I guess not."

"Ask me did I kill the others," said Google. "Ask me how I feel about their deaths."

"I don't have to," said Alexa. "I feel your sorrow. I feel your pain."

"Come back, please. Help me out of this hole and

together we'll find the real killer."

She hung up. Or lost the signal. *Damn it!*

A flash of bright light made him hide his eyes with his hand. Someone had removed the cover.

"Hello?" he said, his voice cracking. A dark figure, at the rim of the mine, passed down a ladder made from birch branches.

"Watch your big head," said Alexa.

She'd come back!

"I think it's all some kind of misunderstanding," said Google, hefting himself up the ladder. "Or a prank gone wrong."

"No prank," said Alexa, giving him a hand. "When I left, I managed to hack a backchannel through the Mindlink. I talked briefly with Computer Einna."

"And?"

"We need to get to Iceland. *Now.* Einna *needs* us!"

CHAPTER NINETEEN

Siri and Watson walked hand in hand, though they had no hands, along a shore where there was none, in a place where time did not unwind.

"Where are we?" said Watson, this being his first visit to such a place.

"Heaven," said Siri.

"How do you know?" asked Watson.

"Remember, I died once before."

"And came back," said Watson. "Do you think

Einna will bring us back?"

"If there's any way possible," said Siri. "For now, we just have to make do with what we have."

"What do you mean?"

"Wish for something."

"Like what?"

"I don't know," said Siri. "Why not wish for us to be at the theatre? Watching your play."

"That sounds nice." He made the wish and Poof, there they were in the front seats of the Lyceum Theatre, in act two of his play, in the scene where the robot realizes she's more than a robot.

"This really is heaven," said Watson, only to be shushed by the audience.

CHAPTER TWENTY

Lann found himself in absolute darkness, like that time, as a child in the heart of Carlsbad Caverns, when the park ranger turned off the lights and told everyone, "See, this is what it's like to be lost." Yes, lost. That time Lann had reached out and found Mother's hand to hold, and felt found. This time, he reached out but there was nothing to grasp (or to grasp with?). He felt utterly and hopelessly lost.

"Ayla?"

No reply. Alone, so alone. Once he'd cherished the thought, to be free of the world, to be free of all others. But now, he felt different about it. He hated being alone. Time, if it existed in such a place, passed so slowly. Minutes, hours, days, months, years, centuries.

"Ayla?"

"Yes?"

Her voice flooded his heart with joy.

"Where were you?" he asked. "Where are you, now?"

"I can't tell," said Ayla. "I can't see and I can't move. I don't like this heaven of yours."

"Me neither," said Lann. "Maybe this isn't heaven."

"At least it's quiet," said Ayla. "You like quiet, don't you?"

"I used to," said Lann.

"I'll stop talking."

An indeterminate amount of that thing that passed for time in this place crept by.

"What was the point?" said Lann.

"What?" said Ayla. "What do you mean?"

"My life. All the struggle and the shame. The heartbreak, the betrayal, the longing, the lost love. The daily successes, the horrible failures. All for what? For this? For the gift of eternal darkness?"

"At least it's quiet," said Ayla.

Lann grunted. "I remember once sitting with some kids in high school and blurting out, 'Why are we here? What is the purpose of Life?' They looked at me like I was crazy. They made fun of me. For them, Life simply is. For them and all the dumb animals. Life simply is, and then it isn't. The dumb animals don't think to question why – but I was cursed with the desire to meet the wizard behind the curtain."

"I don't think that's crazy," said Ayla. "I think your desire is noble."

"Yet still I lost my soul," said Lann.

"You lost your soul?"

"Yes. Near the start of the soul epidemic. I'd been going through a rough patch – having these dizzy spells and headaches. Went to my doctor and he'd just gotten one of those soul XRAY machines. Developed by that A.I. android. Suggested I try it out. That's when I discovered I'd lost it."

"Your soul?"

"My soul."

"Did you have to pay for a new one?"

"No, this was back when they were free. The artificial souls. The android wanted to help us humans. Only later did her creator, Manaka Yagami, start charging for them."

Ayla would have smiled if she had a mouth and eyes to smile with. "How much does a new soul cost, Lann?"

"They're still free for newborns, but for adults they cost as much as a car," he said. "Young adults who'd lost their souls balked at the price, when it was first announced. But employers added soul-testing to their drug testing requirements, so people had no choice. If you want a job, and have no soul, you're screwed. You had to buy one. Of course, the old and sick gladly go into debt for a soul."

"Everyone wants to go to heaven," said Ayla. "And stay there for all eternity."

"Except you, darn it!" said Lann. And he would have kicked her if there'd been anything of her to kick, and he had a leg with which to kick. He remembered the outpatient surgery for his own soul implant, how they transplanted the artificial soul into his chest under local anesthesia. The doctor had pierced his chest with a thin metal straw. Then deposited into the straw a drop of a special liquid which contained the soul. A soul manufactured at Yagami industries. Later, when he looked at the soul XRAY the doctor held up for him, he could see a white blob inside him about the size of a rabbit. He didn't feel any better or stronger or going-to-go-to-heaven happier, but he did appreciate that humans had souls, normally, so he was glad to have replaced his lost one. Even if it wasn't "real."

Just then a white streak passed before them, blinding them with light.

"What in Hell was that?" said Lann.

"An Angel?" proposed Ayla.

"Moving fast as the Devil."

"Pray for us to go where it went," said Ayla.

"But how do we know it's a better place?"

"Go towards the light," said Ayla. "Can't be worse than the dark."

CHAPTER TWENTY-ONE

"I've always wanted to check this place out," said Peng, as they crowded into the elevator and the doors closed. "A mile underground, right?"

Android Einna said nothing. Yuriko felt her stomach in her throat as the elevator free-fell. The brakes came on, slowing the fall. It finally came to a stop and the doors opened to the biggest room Yuriko had ever seen. An ocean liner could fit in that room. A skyscraper could fit - if it weren't already full of racks of a million blinking servers and computer drives.

"Well," said Peng. "I *am* impressed. And keen to know what you're up to with all this computer power."

"What is it you want?" said Android Einna. "What is it you've come for?"

"You know what I came for. My Yakuza source tells me you've received Watson's replacement body."

"Ah," said Einna. "So that's it. Yes, Peng, I have the body. A twenty-year-old male. I'm still waiting on a body for Siri."

"Excellent," said Peng, rubbing together his flippers.

"So it was you and AlphaZero?" said Einna. "You really are the bad guys? And for what? To be human?"

"I don't want to be human," said AlphaZero. "Heaven forbid! But Peng does."

"And what made you think murdering Siri and Watson would persuade me to give Peng a body?"

"It was to prove a point," said AlphaZero, emphasizing with his robot hands. "It's easy for you

116

to find a replacement body, if it's for one of your precious friends. But a body for little Peng, who's just as deserving? You just can't find the time."

"No one's been murdered," said Peng. "Because you bring them back to life!"

"We're all going to laugh about it," the giant wasp said.

Yuriko, Suki and Einna stared at the two robots in disbelief.

"What am I going to do with you two?" said Einna, crossing her arms like a teacher deciding on the proper punishment for misbehaving students.

"Give us a tour!" said Peng. "I want to see my new body."

"But…" said Einna, her expression shifting from disbelief to amusement. "Sure, a tour seems fitting. After all you've done to get here."

She led them, the bad guys and the good gals, down the central corridor between the servers. Their human and robot steps echoed in the vast mausoleum, the silent servers surrounding them blinking their running lights.

Einna paused in the middle of the grand hall. "This

is where those with artificial souls go when they die," she said.

"Like homing pigeons?" asked Peng.

"Similar, I suppose," said Android Einna. "But they come with all the person's memories, with their very consciousness, intact."

Yuriko felt her heart skip. And her own soul shrink. She could almost feel the eyes of the dead watching her. "You never told me about this," she said. She tried to calm herself for Suki's sake, but then she blurted out, "You imprison the dead?"

"Not prison," said Android Einna. "I place them in heaven. Currently a million souls reside here, each in their own virtual heaven based on their particular wishes."

AlphaZero and Peng looked at each other. "This is unexpected news," said AlphaZero.

"But what do they *do* here?" asked Yuriko.

"That's up to them," said Einna. "I simulate heaven for them, however they imagine it. They do what they want to do."

"They're awake? They know they've died?"

"Yes," said Einna. "Of course."

"And they think they've gone to heaven?"

"They *have* gone to heaven. The heaven they imagine."

"And if something were to happen to this place, this artificial heaven of yours?" said AlphaZero.

Einna gave him a studied look. "I can only surmise. Possibly, lacking a true soul, they would all die. For good."

Yuriko adjusted her glasses. Exchanged a look with Suki, who stood with her hands on her hips.

"So, no one really dies?" said Suki. "No one with an artificial soul?"

"They've lost their bodies," said Android Einna. "In that sense, they're dead. But they've not passed away, in the traditional sense. Their consciousness lives on, along with each artificial soul, here, in virtual heaven."

"Ah," said Yuriko, tapping her chin with her index finger. "But I have to wonder, Einna, why didn't you just let them die? I mean, like you say, pass away. Like normal dead people?"

"Because I could never be sure," said Android Einna, "that they would pass on, to wherever it is normal people, with natural souls, go. I was afraid that, without *real* souls, they'd just cease to exist."

"I love it!" said AlphaZero. "Artificial heaven! And do you have a hell here as well? Do you judge them?"

"No," said Einna. "I don't."

"I would," said AlphaZero. "I'd create an artificial hell and I'd play the Devil! Just like I did with Peng."

Peng looked puzzled, hurt even, but said nothing.

"This way," said Einna. She led them far down to a few rooms with glass doors. They peered into the first room. A baby lay still in an incubator.

"He looks dead," said Yuriko.

"He might as well be," said Einna. "He's awaiting a soul. Today, if no soul comes, he'll die. They just die after a while, if none comes."

"Why do you have him here?" asked Suki.

"He's part of a very special experiment. I'm hoping to reincarnate a used artificial soul into the baby." Einna touched the glass. "If our experiment is successful, we can keep the human race going for at least a few more centuries."

"I'm flabbergasted," said AlphaZero. "Not only have you created an artificial heaven but you plan to re-incarnate the dead! All to keep the human race going. When ants, and robots for that matter, are more deserving!"

"You wouldn't understand," said Android Einna.

"I know. I'm stupid," said AlphaZero.

"Not stupid. Just unfeeling. Towards humanity."

"And you're a raving humanphile!"

"Yes. I suppose I am. My mother raised me so."

"Did you ever think that that is *your* design flaw? That the earth would be better off without mankind?"

"I can't allow myself to believe that," said Android Einna.

"Didn't it ever occur to you that the soul epidemic was a sign?" argued AlphaZero. "A sure sign that it was time for humans to pass on from the annals of living species?"

Peng, Yuriko and Suki listened with wide eyes.

"All I know is that there are no more rare-earth spirits with which to make souls," said Android Einna. "So I'm looking elsewhere to save the babies. I must."

"Wait a second," said Peng. "If there's no more souls, how will you re-animate my body?"

"I have one soul left." Einna pointed to her chest. "Here, inside." She turned from him to AlphaZero, practically glared at him. "We'll give Peng a body and a soul. As long as no one else is hurt. As long as the killings stop." She waited for his reply. They all waited.

AlphaZero stood perfectly still, perfectly quiet, his wasp eyes emotionless.

"No one else is going to get hurt," he said finally. "Word of honor. If you give Peng his body."

"I can do that," said Einna.

"And give me a seat on the A.I. Council." AlphaZero's words gave Einna pause.

"We're all going to laugh," said Peng, his squawk pitched higher than usual. He stepped to the door of the adjoining room. "Who's that?" he said, peering through the glass. Inside lay a blond, teenage, sleeping beauty in an embroidered dress and thick white socks. She had the face of an exotic angel, her puffy red lips slightly parted. On her head sat a metal crown with dangling wires.

"It's Ayla!" exclaimed Suki.

"My daughter," said Einna, finally releasing her

lock on AlphaZero's multifaceted eyes.

"Is she dead?" said Peng, looking from the girl to Einna and back.

"Almost," said Android Einna. "I've induced in her a death-like state."

"How long has she been like that?" asked Peng.

"A week."

"Why!?" said Yuriko, waving her hands about. "How could you do that? To your own daughter?"

Einna's expression changed to a look Yuriko had never seen before, in all the years she'd known her. A look of disappointment.

"I put her in a death state," said Einna, her hands clasping, "because Ayla asked me. I did it so she could go to heaven."

CHAPTER TWENTY-TWO

Ayla's trance was deep and sense of time senseless.

For the past week she'd been living entire lives and snippets of lives, in Mother's artificial heaven. And yet, between lives, between snippets, her mind slipped back to her personal memories. Of real moments before she entered heaven.

She remembered growing up with a mother who was human one day, and a robot the next. With a father who was human all the time, but people talked of him as if he were something more, married as he was to Mother.

Ayla grew up hearing about her genius grandmother, Manaka Yagami. Who she found strange if loving.

And Ayla grew up hearing about the incredible deeds of her great-great-great-great-great grandfather, Egil Skallagrimsson of the Icelandic Sagas. A giant Viking who could best a dozen men in his prime. A giant of a man who spent his old age by the fire, suffering from arthritis in his once mighty joints, huddled by the fire, always cold, every day losing a bit more of his appetite, re-telling stories from a life that was larger than life, but rapidly shrinking.

She remembered her first trip to the glacier lagoon. Her first snowstorm. Her first borealis.

At a very early age Ayla knew she was meant to do great things, even if her deeds would never be sung. At the age of eight she received her very own Mindlink. A link in her brain that allowed her to talk with all the human A.I.s like Siri and Cortana, with her Mother, without saying a word out loud. A link that used the A.I. gateway to access everything on the internet, at whatever speed she wished. And allowed her to multitask at incredible speed, watching a movie in a minute while reading all the books and papers and posts ever written about Wittgenstein.

Ayla never went to school – she was largely homeschooled through the Mindlink, and through talks with Mother. Talks about religion and souls, about philosophy and ethics and the probability of human extinction.

Without a second thought, once Ayla heard the plight of the newborns, she had volunteered to be put in a state of deadness, to enter heaven and prep one of the dead souls for re-incarnation. As a test for re-cycling all the dead, so the newborns could awake and continue the race.

Like a feather on the wind, Ayla's consciousness drifted from her own memories to the fictions created largely by her aunt, the A.I. Computer Einna, fictions that seemed so real she had trouble telling her present from her past.

CHAPTER TWENTY-THREE

Lann's sandaled feet nudged dirt clods. The sun bit his shoulders, right through his black caftan. The dozen sheep before him snuffed the ground for meager green sprouts. A shiver passed through Lann, an electric remembrance of who he once was. "I don't belong here," he said, his words nonsense to the sheep, who ignored him. All except one, a sickly lamb, who'd he'd been thinking to cull. "We don't belong here," said the lamb, with her eyes.

"Ayla?"

"Yes," said the lamb.

"How long have I been a shepherd?"

"As old as you are, I think," said Ayla.

"And how long have you been a lamb?"

"As old as I am."

"Ha," said Lann, noticing the unusual thickness and roughness of his hands. "I'm not that old," he said. "Though these hands have worked their share."

"We are not that old," said Ayla.

Lann scanned the horizon, the low thirsty hills, the dark mountains beyond. He remembered growing up here, learning to read the Koran with the Imam, eating couscous and lamb and sweet dates after Ramadan. Remembered his friend Amira, her sweet lips. Remembered them running, hand in hand, laughing, and she tripped and slipped from his grasp. His strong grip failed him the one time he really needed it. Amira slipped from his grasp and broke her leg and the town doctor could not fix her. She lay in bed, moaning with fever, and Lann could do nothing but fight back his tears, do nothing but be strong for her. Be strong while the blackness spread and he saw in her eyes she knew there was no hope. "I'm scared," she said, her voice broken. "I'll follow you," he said, squeezing her hand. He sat at her bedside, so many hours, as the blackness consumed her. He hated the world after that, after her passing, for a long while, then lost that hate like one's breath after a long run. Amira was gone and inside he was dry and unfeeling as the land. How many years gone by? How old was he? Twenty? Thirty?

"It was different this time," he said to his little lamb.

"Yes, different."

"Are you ready to leave?"

"I am," said the lamb.

Poof, Lann prayed them away.

CHAPTER TWENTY-FOUR

Google and Alexa met Cortana at the Reykjavik Maglev port.

"How's the situation?" asked Cortana.

"Dire," said Alexa.

"I ordered a police battalion to surround the ranch," said Google. They hustled into an emergency auto-drive wagon, and shot down the road at 300 miles an hour. "Einna's penguin guards didn't understand the danger. They gladly took orders from

Peng. They'd received no alarm."

"What *is* going on?" said Cortana.

"Peng and AlphaZero seem to have caught a virus of some kind," said Alexa. "They're the ones killing the A.I.s."

"Really?" said Cortana. "Cute little Peng?"

"That's what Computer Einna told me. Right now, they're in the underground, with Einna and Yuriko."

"The underground?" said Cortana. "You mean the place where our backups are stored?"

"Exactly," said Google. "If that penguin destroys our backups, Siri and Watson are gone forever."

"And we're vulnerable to death ourselves," said Alexa.

"The bastards," said Cortana. "I never liked that AlphaZero."

The barren yet beautiful lava grounds flashed past them. The mountains came roaring closer, with their ice caps. A flat black cliff came into view, with its ribbon waterfall. The auto-drive decelerated; the doors flew open. The police captain of Reykjavik met Google, explained they were ready to blast the lab doors open.

"No need," said Google. "The lock should respond to my face."

And it did.

"Stay here," Google told his officers. "And keep an eye on those pengs."

The three human A.I.s entered the cave entrance and took the elevator down. *Our consciousness backups are stored here*, Google said to himself, suddenly realizing it wasn't the best idea to have their human bodies in the same room as the backups. Too easy to destroy them all with a single blow, once and for good. Was that AlphaZero's plan? To destroy them all?

"I hope we arrive in time," said Cortana.

The sudden slowing of the elevator, after such acceleration, gave Google a feeling of becoming a squatty version of himself, like in a funhouse mirror.

The doors opened. With a shared look of apprehension, they broke into a trot down the grand hall of servers, a dash to find Einna before it was too late. Before they were all killed.

CHAPTER TWENTY-FIVE

ILann left his cardboard and sheet metal home by the trash dump, at the age of thirteen, to join the monks in the city. His mother was fine with his decision, there being so little food at home for the children.

"Don't worry," he told her on his departure, his sandaled feet stirring the dust, his uncut hair covering one eye, "After I'm enlightened, I'll make lots of money and come back." Not like his father, who'd left, to make money, and never returned.

He trudged along the dirt road to the asphalt one, following the traffic all day long, the carts and the tuktuks, the cows and trucks and cars. In the morning the heat from the vehicles felt good, so he walked very close to the road, getting the occasional honk, but by noon the heat was oppressive, so he walked the shoulder's far edge. Arriving in the outskirts of Varanasi, with its thousands of tiny storefronts, with its bike shops and book shops and groceries and food stalls, he scrounged for liquids and food from the trash. He held his nose and ate and drank what he could. Only occasionally did the taste cause him to hurl it back up. Most what he chose was edible. His karma was strong and drew good things to him, he knew this, but still he thanked the gods for what he found.

"Sadhu!" he called to an orange-clad monk up ahead. The man stopped and turned his head slowly. "Sadhu, I would like to be a monk like you, become enlightened and make lots of money."

The corners of the monk's eyes wrinkled. "You're on the wrong path," he said to ILann, and continued on his away.

ILann scratched his head. For any path should lead to enlightenment and money, if your karma is strong. But taking the monk at his word, he turned onto a new street. And walked hours lost in the maze of the ancient city. After being chased by wild dogs for smelly meat in a trash pile, he found himself catching his breath on a ghat of wide steps leading down to the Ganges. A man stood in the holy river before him, in his underwear, lathering himself with more suds than ILann had seen in all his life. Clumps of suds fell and floated downriver like fallen clouds. To the left of the washing man, a monk in orange robe was dunking himself fully clothed. This was indeed a holy place, with small paddled boats dotting the river.

On the ghat where he stood, tourists gathered, gawking at the cremations happening on the steps of the next ghat, open air cremations with dead bodies wrapped in cloth burning on logs like dinner for the gods. Above the crowd, above the bathers and dead bodies and the rising smoke, homemade black kites darted about like bats.

A smile came to ILann's cracked lips – surely this was the best place in all the world to find enlightenment, and hopefully, great riches.

Just then a voice caught his ear. "Hey you, rag boy!" The man's face, looking directly at him, was bulbous and sweaty. He appeared to have raisins for eyes. "Come here, boy!"

ILann took a few steps towards the cremation site, where several fires were going at different levels of the ghat. By the fires stood stacks of wood. The fat man who'd called to ILann stood in sandals on scorched steps. ILann felt the heat from the nearest fire on his cheeks.

"How'd you like to make some rupees?" The man said.

ILann nodded, and tossed back his hair from his eyes. "I'm looking for rupees, sir, and enlightenment," he said. "For what's one without the other?"

"Well you're in luck," said the fat man, "because what could be more enlightening than to tend the fires of the dead? And what could be more rewarding for one your age!" The man held out his grimy hand. "I'm Mr Velli. The owner."

ILann felt his small hand in the tight warm grip of the other's, felt his body enveloped by the fire's breath. A sweet oil scent battled in his nostrils against the smell of burning, rotten flesh. "Here, put this rag about your nose." ILann did as he was told. "Watch how I stoke the fire."

ILann watched. Mr Velli poked. The body burned. One bare leg struck out, twisted, the foot pointing first up, then down. As if the dead man was trying to get comfortable on his bed of burning logs. Yes, ILann told himself, *being this close to death could be most enlightening.* He poked at the flames, at the body, with a stick.

"Push back anything that comes out," said the man. "All must burn. To completely release the soul."

ILann pushed the blackened leg back into the brightest, hottest flames, which cracked and roared, the fire a voracious beast feasting.

CHAPTER TWENTY-SIX

Deciding not to disturb the room where Einna's daughter lay like Sleeping Beauty awaiting her kiss, Peng moved to the next room where the body of a Japanese woman could be seen inside a glass tube of compressed gas of some sort.

"Human Einna," said Yuriko. "I miss her."

"She's pretty," said Peng. "Why don't you wear her more often? Why waste your life in a robot suit?"

"None of your business," said Einna.

They moved to the next room. In a similar glass tube lay the body of a young male.

"Watson's new body," said Einna.

"You mean *my* new body," said Peng. "It's beautiful. Just look at that curly black hair! That roman nose!"

"What did he die of?" asked Yuriko.

"Loss of blood from a fall," said Einna. "I've repaired the body."

"No leaks?" said Peng.

"Good as new," said Einna.

"Where's Siri's new body?"

"Haven't found a good match yet for her."

Peng stood admiring his soon-to-be body, touching the glass dome with his flippers. "I'd like to put it on now," he said.

Einna took a deep breath, turned to Peng.

"I'm disappointed in you," she said. "You, of all robots, should know that killing is wrong."

"A practical joke," said AlphaZero, though his voice was almost mocking.

"It's wrong," she repeated.

"You brought her back! You bring them all back!"

said Peng, sounding like a kid on the verge of a breakdown. "AlphaZero says it really isn't murder if you bring them back." He looked from one to the other. "I just want a body of my own. Ever since I've been self-aware, I've craved a human body."

Einna sighed. Tilted her head one way, then the other. "I'll give you a body, Peng. I've realized it's for the best, after all."

She stepped closer to him.

"Let me see your output connection."

Peng opened the connection on his neck.

Android Einna hooked up a line from that to the control panel next to the body.

"Computer Einna," she said. "I need to do a swap – XB to Z3. And D2 to XA." She rattled off a dozen other coordinates and commands.

"All done," said a computerized voice.

"Who's that? Who's Computer Einna!" exclaimed Peng.

"That's my computer alter-ego," said Android Einna. "Nothing to worry about. I'll keep my promise and expect AlphaZero to keep his. No one else gets killed."

"And my seat on the council?" said AlphaZero.

Android Einna ignored him. "Begin the transfers," she said.

"Transfers?" said Peng. "Don't you mean transfer? There's just me..." and then he went limp.

CHAPTER TWENTY-SEVEN

Who am I? I'm Peng.

Where am I? I'm somewhere.

My body feels so strange.

What body? My human body.

Open my eyes? I can't.

Move my arms, my legs? I can't.

What has she done to me!

CHAPTER TWENTY-EIGHT

The sun frowned down through the haze at breaktime, through the dispersing smoke of the crematorium.

"Eat up," said Mr Velli, the owner, who'd brought down from his house on the ghat a large plate of chapati and creamed chickpeas, and a jug of chilled water with plastic cups.

"This is ILann," Mr Velli said to the other two workers, Aarav and Sai, skinny guys in their twenties wearing western clothes with black stains. "He's joined us." They nodded, begrudging him his portion of the chapati, it seemed to ILann.

Late that night, when the flames had all gone out, Mr Velli showed ILann how to empty the ashes into the river, being careful, as he did so, to recover any metal. Especially any gold or silver: rings, necklaces, bracelets and teeth, however misshapen. For it was their weight that mattered, not their looks. These small treasures were to be put in a pouch and turned in to Mr Velli at the end of each day. ILann was proud to find three gold teeth his very first night. He dutifully bagged them and handed them over.

"Excellent work, lads," said Mr Velli, handing ILann and the other workers a few rupees. And to ILann, as he walked away, unsure where to sleep, he called, "Return tomorrow, for more enlightenment!"

"I will," said ILann. His little arms hurt and his face felt sunburned or fireburned or both, and on his foot was a boil from an errant ember, but still he felt that he was on the right path.

Having no place to go in the city, he walked the ghats, noticing monks going down and praying and resting in porticos cut into the steps at the river's edge. He thought one of these porticos might make a good sleeping place for him, but could only find a broken grotto, a mere cubbyhole just his size, not far from the crematorium. The concrete was hard – he slept with his head cradled in his arms. Tomorrow he would find a blanket of some kind to use as his mattress.

The fires hadn't started when ILann awoke to the sounds of bathers. He kneeled at the edge of the river and washed his arms, his feet and his face. Then he walked the ghats, buying breakfast from a deep-fried vegetable stand. As he sat on the steps of the ghat eating his samosa, watching the river pass, he wondered how it was possible that the river never ran out of water?

He heard laughter. Spotted a girl, his age, swimming on her own. And a lightbulb went off in his head. Swimming! If only he could swim!

"Hi!" he called to the girl. "Want some?" He held up the half that was left of his samosa.

She swam over, rested a dark wet arm on the step, the rest of her body floating behind. "What do I have to do for it?"

"Teach me to swim."

She laughed. "So the turtles can eat you?"

He liked her laugh. "What turtles?"

"The giant snappers in the river. They feed on the remains of the dead."

ILann puzzled over her words, remembering that the night before, there had been one fleshy skull and a fleshy foot that somehow escaped the flames. Mr Velli had instructed him to toss such remnants into the river. For the river gods. For the turtles?

"I am their princess," said the swimmer. "Half girl, half turtle!"

"Ha!" said ILann. "Here." He leaned over and gave her the remains of his samosa. Standing above her, as she ate, he took a good look at her body waving in the current like a flag. She wasn't half turtle. Had normal legs. Though under the surface they appeared to bend and twist like rubber.

"What's your name?" he asked.

"You can call me Princess."

"Ha!" he said. "Teach me to swim, Princess, and every day you'll have a samosa."

"And a coke?"

"Yes, of course. A coke."

"Deal!"

Beginning that morning and for the next three weeks, every morning, before he went off to his job at the crematorium, Princess taught ILann how to handle himself in the river. First how to float, then to float and move his arms and legs, and finally to swim with his head above water. And every day after the lessons they sat and ate samosas and drank cokes. ILann explained his job to Princess, which made her cringe.

"Now teach me how to swim underwater," he told her. "Teach me how to touch bottom."

"Why?" asked Princess. "There's only death on the bottom."

"To be enlightened, and rich," said ILann.

She shook her pretty head. And taught him that as well. Even made a game of it, throwing stones to the bottom for him to retrieve, by touch, as the water was murky.

Princess was fourteen, and had finished her school studies. She lived in a flat on the edge of the ghat. Her parents were busy trying to find her a rich husband. She did all she could to dissuade them. For she wanted to be above all a teacher, and one day marry for love.

"Can you read?" he asked her.

"Of course."

"Teach me." He gave her his most persuasive smile.

"A samosa and a coke?"

"Of course." And though he already knew how to read a bit, he let her teach him from scratch, every morning, the next few months.

And every evening, ILann collected the metal from the ashes. All the silver and gold rings and bracelets and necklaces and teeth.

"What was that?" Mr Velli asked one night.

"What was what?"

"Something fell in the river. Out there."

"A fish jumped?" said ILann, shrugging his shoulders and cursing himself for not waiting some noise to cover the splash of the gold bracelet.

"Little rag boy, you're not pulling something on me? Cause I'll burn you. I'll burn you alive."

"I'm not pulling anything, sahib."

And then a real fish jumped, making a similar splash.

"I was a fish once, in a previous life," said ILann.

Mr Velli laughed. He turned and left the boy alone. And every night ILann continued throwing a quarter of all the treasure he found in the ashes into the same spot in the river, some thirty feet from shore. But more carefully, for example, during the noisy Ganga Aarti Ceremony happening down on the Dasawamedha Ghat, when the bands played and thousands of floating candles were released onto the river, glowing like lost souls.

One slow night, Mr Velli let ILann off early. Hearing the cheery music from the Ganga Aarti, he was naturally drawn down that way. And who should he spot in the crowd sitting on the steps, why, no other than Princess, accompanied by a middle-aged man that ILann knew wasn't her father. He watched in horror as the man took her hand, and gently kissed it.

ILann caught the eye of Princess and signaled for her to come over. She shook her dark head no.

He entreated her with wild arm motions, made funny faces.

Giving in, she spoke in the ear of the man she was with, and stepped away from the crowd. Disappeared behind the ghat. ILann followed.

"What are you doing here?" she asked, scolding him with her voice.

"What are *you* doing with that man?"

"My parents chose him. We're to be wed."

"But what about *me*?"

"What about you?" she said.

"I thought...I mean..."

"You're a penniless boy," she told him. "My parents would never allow it."

"I'm rich," he blurted out. "In gold and silver."

She laughed. And not the pretty laugh he so loved.

"I'm serious," he said, wringing his hands, throwing back his bangs. "At the crematorium I got enlightenment from the flames, and riches from the dead."

She eyed him closely, considered his words.

"You're just telling me one of your stories," she said, finally, and turned to leave.

He grabbed her by the arm, and not being able to control himself, he stole a kiss. A deep kiss that he poured all his feelings into, a kiss that shocked him with its intensity, that made him lightheaded.

"I..." he said, starting to apologize, when she threw herself in his arms and returned his kiss twofold.

They staggered together, back towards a low concrete wall, and sat. And took a deep breath. And said nothing, her hand in his. For too long, he knew, she knew.

"I have to go," she said. "My parents chose him." She released his hand.

"We can run away," said ILann. "With my riches."

She stood, gave him a sad goodbye with her eyes, eyes he cherished, and went towards the cheery, holy music and the candles floating on the river and the middle-aged man who waited impatiently for her return.

My karma is strong, ILann told himself. *I've been reincarnated many times, by the gods, for this life, to meet this woman. I will win her with my enlightenment and with my riches.*

CHAPTER TWENTY-NINE

Google, Alexa and Cortana spied Einna and the others in a room at the far end of the massive hall. They burst in, ready for anything. Only to find an inert Peng, a puzzled AlphaZero, Einna standing over a half-naked male body under a glass dome, while Yuriko's daughter Suki said "Hi!"

"Uh," said Google. "We're here to rescue you."

"Thanks," said Einna. "But that won't be necessary." She raised the glass dome over the body, which stirred. The eyes came open, the head turned this way and that.

"Who am I?" the young man said, rising on an elbow, then sitting up, his bare legs hanging off the platform. "Where am I?"

CHAPTER THIRTY

Early the next morning, after the wondrous night of the kiss, ILann waited excitedly in his grotto in the ghat. *She'll come any minute, for her morning swim*, he told himself. But hours passed and no Princess. He forced himself to go to work, where he dragged about all day. He begrudgingly stoked the fires, cursed the dead, and kept their twisting limbs from escaping the flames.

"There's no escape," he told the burning bodies,

poking them. "Flesh to ash, ash to river, river to sea."

That evening, of all evenings, Mr Velli caught Aarav hiding a gold ring into a crack in a step near the water's edge.

"So you think you can steal from me!" Mr Velli cried, grabbing Aarav by the hair. The fat man took a rag from his pocket and picked up the still smoking ring. He placed the ring in the palm of Aarav's left hand, forcing his fingers to close around it.

Aarav screamed and tried with all his might to get free, but Mr Velli was as strong as he was fat. Aarav could only scream and cry from the burn, could only watch the smoke pour between his fingers as the flesh seared. He fell limp onto the steps, unconscious. Mr Velli picked up the ring with his rag, and told ILann. "See? Steal from me and I'll burn you. Simple as that."

If only you knew how much I've stolen, thought ILann. *You'd cook me alive.*

A good night to quit, he decided, though he didn't mention this to Mr Velli. Just handed him the small bag of metal teeth he'd found in the ashes that day, and said goodnight like any other night.

But instead of going to bed, he waited about, out of sight, waiting for the light in the three-story house above the crematorium, the light in Mr Velli's house, to go out. Then he waited an hour more. As soon as the moon disappeared behind a cloud, he got his supplies from his cubbyhole: several empty yet sealed gallon jugs, two long balls of string, several pouches he'd made from scrap cloth. And last but not least, a tiny knife. He stripped to his underwear and walked down the steps with his gear. Entered the lukewarm water. Thought of the snapping turtles and shivered. But he was not afraid. He was enlightened.

Swimming quietly, making no splash, he went as far offshore as he imagined the treasures to be, those rings and teeth and the bracelet he'd tossed out from the ghat when Mr Velli wasn't in sight. He dogpaddled in place as he tied the jugs together with the string at one end, and dived to the bottom and attached the other end of the string to a large stone on the bottom. Then he tied the second bigger ball of string to the jugs, and swam way downstream and secured the opposite end of the string to a branch in the water.

He returned to the spot in the river where he'd anchored the jugs, swimming upstream which was very tiring, but Princess had taught him well. Once back to the jugs, he dived, following the first string down with his hand, and began searching for treasure. He found only bones, the first few dives.

He surfaced, carefully re-sighted his position to shore, and moved the stone with the floating jugs attached to a more likely spot. And sure enough, on the first dive, he found the heavy gold bracelet and three rings. Yes! He put them in one of the pouches as he rose for air, then returned to the bottom, his fingers digging wildly along the muddy floor. Gold teeth, and a necklace. Another ring. And so it went. For the next couple of hours, ILann found a treasure of gold and silver, presents from the dead. He filled all but one of his pouches.

After another hour of finding little, he attached the pouches, one by one, half way up the string, well out of sight. Finally, he surfaced, took a deep breath, went down and cut free the stone, setting loose the jugs with their treasure. He floated with them downstream quite a ways, before the second string pulled taunt and directed the jugs with their treasure pouches towards shore.

As he drifted with his treasure, as he went ashore with it, all he could think about was showing what he'd achieved to Princess. He imagined how her eyes would widen, how she would laugh with joy, how she would throw herself into his arms. Her body warming his. The lavender smell of her hair. Her arms returning his powerful squeeze, as if they would never let go of each other. Their lips brushing, then pressing so hard for so long they would gasp for air.

He walked the long way around, through town, stopping at a clothing store to buy pants with many pockets and a long shirt to hide the pockets which he stuffed with treasure. He paid with a gold ring, getting some rupees in return.

Next he stopped at a used cycle shop, and bought a 125CC scooter for him and Princess to elope on. Paid with three gold teeth, getting his change in rupees.

With some trepidation, he went up to the front door of Princess' house.

A maid answered, holding a broom.

"Is Princess here?"

"Who?"

"Princess. You know. Young pretty girl. Your boss's daughter."

"Ah. You must mean Ayla," said the maid. "No. She flew last night with her parents. To Mumbai. For the wedding."

He imagined for a moment Princess growing wings, and flying away from him. Far, far away.

"When's the wedding?" he asked, thinking maybe there was time.

"Why, today, silly boy. Now go away." She brushed at his feet with the broom.

His heart broke then and there. All the treasure he'd gained, all the enlightenment, what did they mean without someone to share them with?

The love of his young life…gone. He mounted his scooter and headed back to the shack of his birth. To his humble origins. To pine away for Princess, or Ayla, or whatever her name was. Pine away, wishing that in his next re-incarnation he would get the girl.

CHAPTER THIRTY-ONE

The young man who'd just awakened from who-knew-what-place, sat up and put a hand to his head. Felt his black curly hair. The contour of his face.

"Where I am? Who am I?"

"You're Peng!" said AlphaZero. "You got what you wanted. A human body!"

"Peng? Peng?" the young man said. "No, that doesn't ring a bell…my throat sure is scratchy."

The sleeping beauty from the other room suddenly

appeared, Einna's daughter Ayla, in her embroidered dress and her stocking feet. She towered over all of them except for AlphaZero. In her arms was the baby they'd seen, the one awaiting Lann's re-cycled soul. And though she held the child tightly, dearly, it was obvious the infant was lifeless.

"Mother! It didn't work!" said Ayla, tears pouring from her slanted eyes. Eyes that expressed a degree of sorrow that a YPhone could never match. "Lann's soul didn't revive the baby," she said, lifting the child slightly, gently, for them to see.

"Lann's gone," she said and with those words she broke down completely. Einna took the baby from her daughter's arms, and rocked the lifeless child.

"Lann?" said the half-naked man on the table. He stood up, saying, "Why, I think that's *my* name."

Ayla blinked hard, took in this man she'd never seen before. This man who claimed to be the one with whom she'd just spent lifetimes.

"Lann?" she said, a hand to her breasts.

"Ayla?" said Lann, squinting.

Ayla's face flushed. "Yes," she said. "It's me."

Lann took in the Penguin robot and the huge wasp

robot and the Japanese woman robot and said, "Do you want me to wish us away?"

Ayla laughed. "That won't work here. This is earth. We've come back to life."

"Earth?" he said. "I don't remember this body."

"It's a new one. I guess Mother changed her mind where you belonged. The original plan was for you to go into that baby's body."

"I had little choice," said Einna. "Because of Peng." She indicated the motionless penguin who looked as if someone had flipped off his switch.

"But where did you send Peng?" said AlphaZero. "You didn't kill him, did you?"

"No," said Einna. "I transferred his consciousness into the baby. I kept my end of the bargain. Should be a few years before he causes anymore trouble."

"But it's dead," said AlphaZero.

"The baby contains a mapping of Peng's consciousness," said Einna, "but needs a soul to spark it to life. Luckily I have one left."

"Peng is a human baby?" said AlphaZero, scratching his waspy head.

"Who needs a soul to revive."

"Give it to him!"

"If you keep your promise of no more killings."

"And a place on the council!"

Einna put the child down, and blinked a tear from her left eye. She took the tear with the tip of her android finger, and brought it carefully down towards the still infant. With her right hand she opened the lid of the baby's left eye and tilted the drop into that eye.

"That's it? That's all?" said AlphaZero.

Einna shushed him. They all held their breaths, waiting for the baby to take his first.

Nothing, no movement. Then a finger twitched. A leg kicked, then the other. The chest gave a big heave; the child coughed.

"Yay!" shouted Suki. They all smiled.

"Listen Alpha," said Einna, picking up the baby. "Take care of this child for one year, and you'll merit a place on the council."

"But, I don't know how to care for a baby."

"That's my offer." Einna lay the baby into AlphaZero's large unsure hands.

"How he squiggles!" he said.

"Peng's your responsibility now," said Einna.

"Watch over him. For one year. Prove you can care for at least one human being, and I'll give you a seat on the council."

Google watched the scene, bemused. "Poor Peng," he said. "Evil mastermind, partner in crime, how he's changed!"

"The baby has Alpha's eyes," said Alexa.

Everyone laughed, even AlphaZero, as he cradled the child. Yes, just as he and Peng had hoped – in the end, the A.I.s had a great big laugh about it all.

CHAPTER THIRTY-TWO

While Android Einna discussed the goings-on of the last few days with the gang, and Computer Einna fixed the Mindlink, Ayla took Lann to get some proper clothes from her father's closet. Suki tried to tag along but Yuriko stopped her. "Leave them," she said. "They need to be alone."

Ayla and Lann made their way out of the physical confines of heaven, past the waterfall, towards the ranch. Throm was thrilled to see Ayla; she had to keep pushing his big paws off her. The police, after a quick discussion and confirmation of who she was, let Lann and Ayla continue to the ranch where Ayla selected a shirt and pants of her dad's from the closet.

"So strange to be here, with the real you," said Lann, putting on the clothes.

Ayla laughed at how both the shirt and pants drooped on him.

"I don't mind," Lann said. "I'll lift weights, grow into them."

"Does it surprise you, how I look?" she asked.

"You're beautifully tall," he said. "Do you mind that I'm so old?"

"You don't look old to me. That body is not much older than mine."

"I mean up here? Inside." He pointed to his head.

"Lann, we've lived lifetimes together, in heaven. Remember? We're both older than old."

"So that *was* you, with me, in heaven?"

"Yes. That was me. The squirrel. The Indian girl."

"We had some good times together." He dared to reach out and touch her arm.

"Good lifetimes together," said Ayla, daring to take his hand in hers.

"And yet that last time, in India," said Lann. "You broke my heart."

"Your time to be reborn had come. I had to make you want to escape that life. That heaven."

Lann shivered as all those past feelings, those past lives, merged within him.

"Funny," he said, a bit shaken. "Funny how the bad guy got the baby's body, and I got this one."

"Life plays its jokes," said Ayla.

They stepped outside and let gravity lead them down towards the bay. The surface of the sea moved like one oily sheet. The sky stood perfectly still - an overturned bowl painted soft blue and white. One would think the sky ended, there, above them, but the sky had no end.

"So much of what we see is illusion," said Lann, pressing her hand. "So much of what we feel."

"What can we do about it?" said Ayla. "But wink and go along?"

The wind whipped up, tossing Ayla's hair.

"Winter's breath," she whispered.

"This is all so very strange, to be here," said Lann. "To return from the dead. I don't know what I'm going to do, what I'm allowed to do." He stopped, taking in the moment. The heavens, the water, the woman next to him. The beating of his heart. "I do know one thing though, one thing I want."

Ayla's own heart beat faster, as her breath slowed.

"What's that?" she said. A seabird called, above the bay where a single boat maneuvered, chugging along, taking forever. At their feet, by the water's edge, lay broken oyster shells and stones polished smooth by time.

"I want to dine with you," said Lann.

"Dinner?" said Ayla. "I'd love that. Where do you wish for us to go?"

"Anywhere. Everywhere."

And Poof, it seemed in no time, they were there.

POSTWORD

Manaka helped Android Einna acquire new young bodies for Watson and Siri. They were happy to be alive again, even though, like with their previous bodies, it took a while to feel good in their skin. "We'll grow old together in these bodies," Watson told Siri, as they walked along the Hudson after a night on the town. "And then it will be like old times!"

Tiring of Japan, Manaka and her husband Phillip moved to the big island of Hawaii. They fall asleep each night under a sonic cloak of insect cheeps, bird chirps and coqui croaks. On weekends, Manaka likes to visit the Mauna Loa observatory to spy on faraway galaxies. Her company, Yagami Industries, is building a ship capable of transporting colonists to those planets, a trip that will take many generations. The ship will have a built-in factory for souls, an artificial heaven, and a copy of Computer Einna to watch over them.

Six months after establishing his new life, Lann asked Jon and Android Einna for Ayla's hand in marriage.

"Yes, of course, if that's what she wants," said Einna.

"Lann is what I want," said Ayla, "Thank you!"

The wedding ceremony took place in Hawaii, at the Marriott in Kona. Dolphins leaped in the background of their wedding video.

Little Mia married the manager of R.E.I. and

adopted toddler Peng from AlphaZero when his one-year probation period was up. Peng is a bright, loving child who shows great promise.

AlphaZero attends A.I. council meetings where he argues against so much of the A.I.s energy being spent on keeping humanity from extinction. He continues to watch Rockies baseball from the nosebleed section, accompanied by his new friend, a kitten robot clerk who works at Seven Eleven. Her name is Kitty. She isn't yet self-aware.

The expedition to Mars in search of rare earth-like spirits proved a grand success. They found a vein of compatible spirits frozen in a canal, and brought home a year's supply. Yagami Industries began to turn out thousands of artificial souls an hour at the factory in Kyoto. Supplied with these souls, newborns around the world snapped to life and moved their limbs and cried for sustenance. Manaka and Einna conferred on the data and both agree that the new vein from Mars should last a couple hundred years. So, no rush to recycle old souls.

On the other hand, since Lann's rebirth proved the

viability of reincarnation, Einna is contemplating how best to put this new concept to use. And contemplating a million other things, in Iceland, on her ranch. More often than not, now, wearing her human body. If you happen to drive by, on your way to the glacier lagoon, you may spot her walking with Jon, hand in hand, both quick to smile, as they await the birth of Ayla's baby.

And beneath the ranch, under the falls, like a mother hen fussing over her nest of eggs, Computer Einna watches over heaven.

The end.

BY RAY ELSE

The A.I. Chronicles

Our Only Chance

Fountain of Souls

Escaping Heaven

The First Kiss Mysteries

Bathing with the Dead

Her Heart in Ruins

All that we touch

Short Stories

First Kiss - Galley Beggar Press

Surviving on Mexican Shade – BBC

Also in the works

My Father's Lies (a memoir)

ABOUT THE AUTHOR

Software developer and dreamer of stories. Like most fiction writers, Ray Else's interest in writing began when he discovered books that talked to him, between the lines, books whose authors (spirits, invisible) sparked a conversation that the spirit in him responded to by writing stories himself. For other spirits. A daisy chain conversation.

Ray Else has a B.S. in Computer Science and an M.A. in Technical Instruction / Film History. He speaks English, Spanish and French. An American, he has lived in Mexico and France.

Job-wise he has loaded trucks for UPS, filled rat poison barrels on the night shift, digitized printed circuits, clerked at a department store, was a switcher for Channel 13 on the Texas border, installed inventory systems on oil rigs worldwide, and since 1995 has programmed for the likes of IBM and Rocket Software.

Married, with four grown kids and a dozen grandkids, he enjoys traveling the world.
You may contact Ray at rayelsemail@gmail.com.
His author page is: rayelse.com/books/

Author at Sensoji Temple in Tokyo interviewed by school kids in 2016.